WILD EMBRACE

WILDER IRISH, BOOK 11

MARI CARR

This story is dedicated to my mom and her sisters, my inspirations for Riley and Bubbles.

They've spent years trying to teach me me how to decorate my house, grow plants, and cook.
They have failed across the board.

However, they were the best role models I could have asked for when it came to raising my children, showing me that laughter is the best medicine, and proving (through example) that weekly "tea times" are more fun when you serve beer.

PROLOGUE

"You're home early, my dear lass. Did you have a nice time?"

Darcy gave Patrick a noncommittal one-shoulder shrug that pretty much said it all. His youngest granddaughter had just attended her senior prom, and he'd thought her plan was to then do a sleepover at her best friend Brooklyn's house.

"It was okay."

It was only a little after midnight, and Patrick was certain he was the only one still awake in the house. He'd moved in with Darcy's parents nearly a decade earlier, his children concerned about him living alone in the apartment above the pub. He'd assured them he was just fine, but when Aaron and Riley put an addition onto their home and created this lovely little living space just for him, he was hard-pressed to say no. He had missed living with other people, being surrounded by family.

The fact they lived in a ranch-style house and he no

longer had to climb stairs was another big selling feature. His knees had been giving him fits for more years than he cared to admit.

Darcy was still wearing her pale green prom dress, though she was carrying her heels by the straps in one hand.

Patrick, who'd been reading in bed, scooted over and patted the mattress next to him. "Come tell me all about it. I'll bet you were the prettiest girl at the dance."

"Everyone looked really nice." Darcy walked across the room and claimed the spot he'd just cleared for her, sitting with her back resting against the headboard, sighing heavily.

"That's a sad sound, my dear. Did you not have fun?"

Darcy twisted slightly to face him. "No. It really was okay. Just okay. I mean...I thought senior prom was supposed to be this awesome, amazing, romantic thing, but it was just a dumb old school dance in the gym."

"No romance, eh?" Patrick asked, trying to hide his grin. He'd been accused by others in his family of being "a bad influence" when it came to teaching his grandchildren about true love and romance. Those lessons had stuck for all of his twelve grandchildren, of that he had no doubt. But while half walked around with their hearts on their sleeves, like Darcy, the other half—his grandsons Colm and Lochlan leading the charge—*pretended* to consider things like true love bull hockey.

Darcy was determined to find her Prince Charming and live happily ever after. Unfortunately, high school hadn't yielded anything other than frogs.

"It was just a bunch of Christmas lights strung up on the bleachers and cardboard cutouts of the Eiffel Tower and the Louvre."

At his quizzical look, she added, "The theme was 'A Night in Paris'."

"Well, that certainly sounds like it had romantic possibilities."

She shook her head. "It didn't."

"And your date?"

"Mark. He was nice, but...he's not the one, Pop Pop. He doesn't make my heart race or my palms sweaty, and there were no fireworks when he kissed me good night. None of those things you said *you* felt when you were with Grandma Sunday."

Patrick smiled. Oh yeah. He'd definitely been a strong influence in this young girl's life. She was one of his biggest fans when it came to his stories about Sunday and Ireland and the early days of the pub when their children started to come along.

One of his favorite things to do was to tell stories about the past and Darcy was his most avid listener, always asking questions and wanting to hear more. He'd become more descriptive over the years, simply for her. Because Darcy had a vivid imagination, he'd had to work hard, turning his words into pictures in her bright, inquisitive, creative mind. It was never enough for him to say the pub where he'd first met Sunday was a typical Irish pub. He had to describe it, the sights, the smells, the sounds. All of it.

And the same was true of his descriptions of love. He couldn't simply say he'd fallen in love with Sunday after that first kiss. She'd demanded to know how he'd knew, what he'd felt—right down to the sweaty palms and twittery stomach and racing heart—that told him Sunday was the one.

"You're only young, lass. There's plenty of time."

"You always say that, but I've never looked at anyone and felt anything even remotely like love. What if I never do?"

Patrick reached over and patted her cheek affectionately. "You will."

"How can you be sure?"

"Because I know you, my lovely dark-haired girl."

Darcy grinned. Patrick had told her years earlier that her name meant "dark-haired or dark one." In her case, it certainly fit...at least appearance-wise. She'd been born with a head full of deep, rich black curls, the color so completely like Sunday's, it had taken his breath away the first time he'd lain eyes on her.

However, there was no denying the meaning of her name only applied to her hair because there wasn't a speck of darkness in Darcy's soul. She was the very epitome of white, bright light.

Even at only seventeen, he was proud to see the confident, compassionate young woman she'd grown up to be. Darcy was one of those rare souls who could look into a person's eyes and see what they needed, be it a joke or a hug or even just someone to sit next to them so they didn't feel so alone.

He saw bits and pieces of his beloved Sunday in all his children and grandchildren, but it was Darcy who seemed the most like his much-missed wife, who'd always been wise beyond her years.

"You know what you want, lass. You've always known."

She nodded. "I want a man like you and Dad. Someone who'll let me be myself, who'll make me laugh, who wants kids, and who'll be so good to them. Someone who will love me forever and never let me go because he can't imagine a day without me in it."

"That is the best list I've ever heard. You deserve all that and more, sweet girl."

She gave her grandfather a kiss on the cheek.

"I've seen your heart, lass. It's far too big to ever live without love. You are so much like my Sunday. Not only in looks, with that beautiful long dark hair, but inside as well. Heaven only knows where I would have ended up if not for Sunday, latching on to me and refusing to let go until I—if you'll pardon the expression—pulled my head out of my ass."

"Wait. You always said you fell in love with her the first night you met her."

"And I did. But falling in love doesn't pave the way to an instant happy ending. That takes hard work, trust, commitment. The truth is...I tried to walk away from Sunday."

Darcy's eyes widened. "Why?"

"Well, she had another suitor, Connall, a man of immense wealth. I knew he could provide for Sunday, could show her the world in a way I never could. In our small village, he was a prince, while I was the pauper."

"So what?" Darcy's tone, her aghast expression, reminded him so much of Sunday's response at the time, all those lifetimes ago, that it took him a moment to gather his thoughts and respond.

"I rather thought I was being selfless at the time. Sacrificing my own happiness for hers because I truly believed I was not worthy of her. She deserved more...always."

"Wow, Pop Pop." Darcy rolled her eyes and Patrick couldn't help but laugh.

"Your grandma Sunday had the same response, which

proves to me you're smart enough to spot the right young man for you. Men aren't always the wisest when it comes to matters of the heart. We tend to think more with our heads and with our pride, which is why we need strong, loving women like you in the world. To show us the error of our ways and guide us to the place we were always meant to be. Your heart will recognize the man who is right for you, just as Sunday's recognized me."

"You think so?" she asked.

Patrick bounced his pointer finger off her perky nose playfully. "I know so. And like you, with those rolling eyes— you get that from your mother, Riley, who got it from *her* mother—Sunday set me straight and let me know that money and happiness did not go hand in hand."

"She didn't give up on you." Darcy hadn't asked it as a question, but he answered anyway.

"No. She didn't. She outsmarted me."

Darcy grinned widely. "How?"

"Oh, in that age-old way all women make the men in love with them face the truth. She tempted the green-eyed monster from his lair by accepting an invitation to a dance from Connall. It soon became obvious I wasn't as selfless as I liked to think. In fact, I was a downright caveman. The only thing I managed not to do the night of the dance was beat my chest and spirit Sunday away over my shoulder in true King Kong style."

Darcy laughed. "I would have loved to see that."

"Yeah. Well, I'm not so sure Sunday would have appreciated that response the night of the dance. She let me know in no uncertain terms that I'd hurt her by trying to push her away. It was then I knew she was meant to be mine, and I vowed to never fail to appreciate the gift I'd been given. Sunday had given me her whole heart and I accepted the value of that priceless treasure, vowing to keep it safe. Sunday was worth more than all the riches on Earth. As are you, my lass. Never give up on your heart's true love. Never settle for a man who doesn't realize exactly how special, how extraordinary you are."

"I won't," she said. "I promise."

He smiled and gave her a kiss on the brow. "Do that, and I promise you will find everything you want. Happiness, romance, and true love."

CHAPTER ONE

Darcy stood up when she heard a car door slam, the sound of voices coming from outside the house. Drifting to the front window, she saw Ryder Hagen emerging from the back of a car, thanking the driver. She spotted the familiar logo of a rideshare company emblazoned on a side window.

She couldn't understand why Ryder was getting a cab home. He'd clearly driven his car to work this morning, given the fact it wasn't in its usual spot in the driveway.

Maybe it broke down?

Then she watched him stumble slightly on the sidewalk, and the light went on. Ryder was drunk. While she'd only babysat for him a dozen or so times in the past year, she'd never seen him drunk.

She listened to him struggle to get his key in the lock for a moment before she realized he needed help. She walked over and threw the dead bolt for him, opening the door.

"Oh, hey, Darcy." He peered over her shoulder but didn't walk into the house. "Boys asleep?"

She nodded. "Yeah. For a couple hours now."

"Good. Don't want them to see me like this."

She grinned, stepping aside as he entered. The two of them had a standard end-of-night routine that all took place in the front foyer of the house. He'd offer her money, she'd reject it, he'd insist, calling it beer money for college, and then she'd take it and head home.

So she was surprised when he walked right by her and straight to the family room.

Darcy paused for a moment, wondering if she should follow or leave. She really didn't need or even want to be paid to take care of the boys. She'd do it for free, something she'd told Ryder over and over again. They were amazing kids, and she enjoyed spending time with them. She could simply call out good night, grab her coat, and be on her merry way. However, the Collins' curiosity gene won out in the end, so she shut the door, following in his wake.

Ryder had dropped down into the recliner, and she suspected he was only a few minutes away from passing out. She'd recently moved into the apartment above her family's business, Pat's Irish Pub, so she was pretty familiar with the stages of intoxication, having witnessed all of them in some form or another in the patrons.

"Do you need anything?" she asked. "Water? Coffee?" She started to include aspirin on her list because she had a feeling his head was going to hurt like hell in the morning, but she didn't necessarily want to point out she could tell he was wasted.

Ryder glanced over, frowning, and she got the sense he

hadn't remembered she was there. He shook his head. "No. Nothing to do but sleep it off. How were the boys?"

"Good as gold, as always. Clint had a little bit of a stomachache after dinner, but I gave him some ginger ale and rubbed his tummy and it passed quickly."

She grinned, completely aware that Clint was faking the stomachache. It was something he'd done quite a few times when she was here.

"His mom always used to rub his stomach when he was sick."

Darcy had come to that same conclusion, which was why she never questioned Clint's illnesses, and instead gave him as much motherly love as she could. "My mom did the same for me."

Ryder closed his eyes briefly. "He misses her," he mumbled.

"That's only natural."

His only response was a grunt.

"I started reading *Harry Potter* to them, but they informed me that your British accent was better than mine."

His eyelids lifted, and she sensed he was trying to focus on her and her comment. "I used to read that to..."

Ryder didn't finish his thought, but he didn't have to. She'd been offering to read the book to them for the better part of a year, but both boys insisted Ryder was reading it to them. Or at least, he had been before his wife died. Darcy couldn't help but notice every time she babysat that the bookmark never moved.

Tonight, Clint was the one to pull it out, and she knew he'd given up hope that his dad would get back to it.

"Vince claims you're the best when it comes to doing Hagrid's voice." Then, she added, "Bloody 'ell, 'arry."

Ryder shook his head, one corner of his mouth quirking up in amusement. "I think that's an Australian accent."

She sighed. "Damn. That's what Vince said too. So, um... I thought you were working late tonight."

When he'd called this morning to see if she was available to stay with his son, Clint, and stepson, Vince, he had mentioned something about a big project at work and his plans to "burn the midnight oil."

"Yeah. I was. Made it all the way to six o'clock before that plan fell through." His words were slightly slurred.

"Fell through?"

"Couldn't concentrate."

This was hands down the longest conversation she'd ever had with Ryder. And she was about ninety-nine percent sure he wouldn't remember it tomorrow. His eyes were clouded, unfocused, and while he was talking—mumbling—he wasn't looking at her, but instead at some random spot on the wall over her left shoulder.

Part of her thought she should probably just leave, but she could tell he was upset, and that bothered her. A lot. Darcy hated it when people were sad, and Ryder Hagen had been sad since the day she'd met him.

Granted, that first meeting had taken place just a few days after his wife, Denise, had been killed in a car accident. He'd spent the last year grieving.

She looked toward the front entrance, then she perched on the edge of the couch.

"Why couldn't you concentrate?" she asked quietly.

"It's Denise's birthday."

"Oh."

Denise and Ryder had been married for six years, buying this house and raising Vince and Clint together. Darcy couldn't even begin to imagine the pain and loneliness Ryder must feel without her.

Nowadays, Ryder shared the place with Leo, their living situation what Darcy considered the most incredible thing two dads had ever done for their kids.

Leo was Vince's dad, so when Denise died, he got full custody of his son. Rather than separate the boys after their mother's death, Leo and Ryder had decided to become roommates to allow the brothers to remain together. They'd already lost their mother, and the men didn't think it was right to also rob the boys of each other.

When her cousin Yvonne, who was good friends with Leo, told her what the men were doing, Darcy vowed she would help them however she could. She wanted this unintentional but wonderful family of all males to succeed. Yvonne had felt the same way, so now they were both pretty regular visitors to the house. Darcy, who was in her last year of college, babysat, while Yvonne—the greatest cook on the planet after Darcy's mom, Riley—brought them dinner a couple times a month.

Ryder leaned his head back against the recliner, his gaze traveling toward the ceiling as he chuckled miserably. "Fucking remembered it this year."

Darcy bit her lower lip, uncertain how to respond. She'd never heard Ryder curse. So between him dropping the F bomb and getting bombed, she was floundering a bit.

"I'm sorry," she said, simply because she didn't know what else to say.

"Always forgot it," he said to the ceiling. "Every fucking year. Woke up this morning and it was the first thing I thought of. She would have been twenty-nine."

Darcy swallowed heavily as a wave of sadness washed through her. She couldn't imagine dying so young, and as she considered the boys sleeping soundly down the hall, she felt incredible sorrow for the entire family. For the boys growing up without a mother, the husband without a wife, and for Denise as well. She was going to miss so much of her children's lives—from birthdays, to Christmases, to graduations, and weddings. It just wasn't fair.

"Ryder—" she started, but he was still muttering, and she was sure he hadn't even heard her speak.

"Every year. Same fight."

She considered his inebriated state and hoped he'd at least spent the evening drowning his sorrows with a friend. No one this sad should be alone.

"Where did you go tonight?" she asked, trying to distract him from the undeniable guilt he was suffering.

"Bar near work."

"Anyone go with you?"

He shook his head, though that was probably not an accurate description. It was more like he flopped it to the left just once before resuming his intense study of the ceiling. "No one...there's no one..." The rest of his sentence was incoherent as he closed his eyes again, breathing deeply.

She considered nudging him, trying to help him move from the recliner to his bed, but she decided against it.

Instead, she stood up and walked over to him. He was still fully dressed in one of his tailored work suits. He'd loosened the tie a bit, but she was certain he wouldn't be comfortable sleeping like that, and she was a bit worried about leaving him in his current state.

Darcy glanced toward the front door again and debated going home. If she weren't here, Ryder would have already passed out, which was pretty much inevitable and probably the best thing for him.

Then she decided against it. Bending toward him, she slowly, carefully untied the knot of his tie, then pulled it from the collar of his shirt.

Ryder grumbled a bit but didn't stir.

Then she reached for the top button of his shirt. She'd just slipped it free when she realized his eyes were open... and he was looking right at her.

"I thought you'd be more comfortable if I loosened your collar," she whispered.

"Don't stop," he said.

Darcy blinked a couple times, then did as he'd asked—actually, commanded was a better word. She'd never noticed how deep and sexy his voice was. Tonight, it had an almost gruff quality to it that was taking her mind to some pretty naughty places.

She unbuttoned his shirt as far as she could, then tugged the hem free of his pants so she could take care of the bottom two. Her fingers accidentally grazed his bare stomach.

She heard him suck in a deep breath.

"I...miss...fuck. I can't..." He turned his head away, and Darcy got the sense he'd gone somewhere else, that he was *with* someone else.

"You miss Denise?" she whispered.

His gaze flew back to hers, his eyes narrowed in a scowl. "No. Yes. I just...can't..." He rubbed his forehead wearily.

"Jesus," he muttered when his eyes briefly managed to focus on her. "Darcy?"

Darcy cursed herself, afraid she'd overstepped a line. She and Ryder weren't close. Hell, they were barely more than strangers.

"I'm sorry. I should probably go," she said softly.

"No. I'm sorry. I..." He squinted hard, as if his head was already starting to hurt. "I don't usually drink. Too much Scotch."

"It's okay. I live above a pub. I've seen my uncles and cousins taken down by Jameson more times than I can count."

The tips of his mouth actually curved upwards, something Darcy took as a win. Ryder wasn't an unpleasant man at all, but he never smiled, and she wasn't sure she'd ever heard him laugh.

The second that thought crossed her mind, she realized she wanted to find a way to bring laughter back to him, to this house.

Clint and Vince had spent the last year talking about how much fun Ryder was, about the games they'd played, the funny voices he used to do when reading stories, how he used to make up silly songs to get them to eat or take a bath. It wasn't until a few months ago that Darcy realized all those stories were about the time before Denise had died. Since then, in addition to rubbing Clint's upset stomach, she'd taken to making up her own songs and doing her own crazy voices to entertain the boys during story time, though apparently, she was going to have to work on her British accent.

Her heart ached for all of them, and Darcy longed to meet the guy Ryder used to be.

Ryder shifted on the recliner and his shirt parted, revealing more of his bare chest. She fought hard to keep her eyes on his face, rather than let her gaze drift lower. Though she'd seen enough when she was unbuttoning his shirt to wish she had the courage to sneak another peek. Ryder was ripped, like six-pack-heaven ripped. He'd mentioned once that there was a gym in the building where he worked that was available to everyone at his company.

Obviously, Ryder took advantage of that. Frequently.

Ryder distracted her when he attempted to unfasten his belt. His fingers fumbled over the clasp several times before she finally pushed his hands away and took over. She unhooked it and then—like she did with his tie—pulled it free.

Darcy started to set the belt on the coffee table, but he grasped her wrist and took it from her.

"Used to..." he muttered, drifting away from her again as he wrapped the leather around one palm.

"Used to?" she asked, confused until her eyes locked on the way he'd distractedly begun to flip the tail end of the belt against his thigh.

Suddenly, a wide array of erotic uses for the belt sprung to mind, and Darcy began to feel hot. Flushed.

Jesus. Aroused.

Between his bare chest, his sexy, deep voice, and the way he was holding that belt, Darcy was letting her imagination travel to places where it had no business going.

"Um. I should—"

Before she could say "go," Ryder spoke again, the words still slurred and halting.

"Everything's...gone." Darcy was unable to follow

anything he was saying, too many of the words mumbled sounds without meaning. "I'm—*mumble*—wish I could —*mumble*—she—*mumble*—now I can't..." Almost all the words he spoke were indecipherable.

Darcy studied his face, quiet in case he tried to finish what he was saying—his mind clearly bombarded by too many things he couldn't deal with—but his eyes were closed again. She couldn't begin to follow his line of thought, mainly because he was losing his battle to remain awake and his slurring was worse.

Her heart cracked as she thought about the pure desolation in his tone. Though an entire year had passed, it was obvious Ryder was still every bit as devastated over losing Denise as he had been the day she'd died.

She longed to find a way to tell him he still had so much to live for. So many wonderful things. This home, the boys, a good job, Leo.

Not tonight, of course. He was too far gone—from the alcohol, the guilt, and the grief.

Darcy had come to love this family very much over the past year. Clint and Vince were sweet, creative, funny kids, while Ryder and Leo were kind, attentive, loving dads. Despite all of that, there was definitely a hole in this home, left behind when Denise died.

She reached for his hand and gave it a gentle squeeze. "It's going to be okay. I'm going to help you."

His eyes didn't open this time, so she went for broke. She untied and pulled off his shoes, then she grabbed a throw blanket from the back of the couch and covered him up.

Ryder slept through it all, breathing deeply, easily.

The alcohol had finally won, finally taken him down.

She took one last look at him before turning off the lights in the family room and quietly walking to the front door.

Just before she left, she glanced back toward where Ryder slept...and her heart gave a funny pang. Darcy had dated a lot of guys the past few years, but she'd never been in a serious relationship. Her sister, Sunnie, teased her, calling her a hopeless romantic, just like Pop Pop. Darcy insisted there wasn't anything wrong with holding out for the right guy, and she'd always been certain that just like Pop Pop, she'd know the minute she met him.

That was when Darcy felt it.

The twittery stomach.

The racing heart.

The sweaty palms.

"Oh no," she whispered to the silent house.

CHAPTER TWO

Three years later...

"What are you still doing here?"

Darcy looked up from her computer, slightly bleary-eyed. She'd been staring at the screen for way too many hours.

She blinked a few times before she was able to clearly see Ryder standing next to her desk.

Wow. She must have been in the zone if she hadn't seen him approaching. Typically, her Ryder radar was much stronger, detecting the man from a million paces away.

She took a deep breath and reached for what she called her Ryder tone—casual, nonchalant, fake as fuck. She'd had three years to perfect it, so as always, she nailed it. "Finishing up a design for Helen. She needs it for Monday's meeting."

"Darcy. It's after nine o'clock. You were here before me this morning. No one expects you to work these long hours."

She grinned, secretly pleased he'd noticed. It meant he'd noticed *her*.

Ryder had a reputation—well-earned—as a workaholic. There were very few days he wasn't the first to arrive and the last to leave the office. Of course, as Vice President of Stadium Operations for the M&T Bank Stadium, Ryder's list of job duties was endless.

She'd just recently been hired as a graphic artist in the marketing department, thanks to Ryder putting in a good word for her with the manager. She was grateful to him for going to bat for her and determined to prove she could handle her first real—benefits and a 401K—job.

Especially since it meant she got to work on the same floor of the same building with him, every single day, instead of just seeing him on the all-too-rare occasions lately when she babysat.

She had known Ryder Hagen for three years, eleven months, and twenty-seven days. And she'd been absolutely obsessed with him for too much of that.

Not that the man had a clue about her crush.

God, she hated that word.

Today marked the end of her second month on the job and, while she loved what she did, she was still struggling to acclimate to the heavy workload. Helen, her department manager, assured her things would ease up a bit once football season was over, but there were still several months to go until February.

"I'm almost finished," she said.

Ryder stepped closer, bending over to look at the screen, and she sucked in a deep breath, catching the faint smell of his musky, woodsy cologne. "That looks fine," he said. "What's left to do?"

"Fine?" she asked, disappointed, leaning back in the

chair and suddenly thinking her design must suck worse than she'd thought. Darcy was her own worst critic, typically stressing over everything from shading to fonts to filters.

Ryder breathed out a long sigh. "Good? Great? Fill in a word, Darcy, then save that and shut down the computer. It's late."

"Wow. High praise," she muttered. "Don't overwhelm me."

"Darcy," Ryder said in a tone he seemed to have reserved just for her. The only way she could describe it was reluctant amusement.

When she'd first started working here, she realized no one in the office spoke to Ryder like he was a real person—no jokes, no teasing, no easy banter, or camaraderie.

Instead, the other employees were all business around him. It wasn't that Ryder was an unreasonable or unkind boss. He didn't yell or scream. In fact, he was very fair and straightforward, but he didn't grab a sandwich with other people in the office or join in on the occasional happy hour or even gab by the coffeepot for a few minutes each morning.

Instead, Ryder put out "keep your distance" vibes. Though Darcy wasn't sure he was aware he was even doing it. It was actually those vibes that called to her because she felt like there was something behind them—sad or wounded. And there was something in Darcy's genetic makeup that couldn't stand to see him always alone at work, because she didn't get a sense that was what he truly wanted.

"I just need another minute or two to—"

"Don't you have a party or something tonight?"

"Shit." Darcy bounced out of her chair so fast, she nearly

coldcocked Ryder with the top of her head. Luckily, he moved away fast, or she would have given him a black eye.

"Oh, Ryder. I'm so sorry. Um. What time did you say it was?"

"Nine," he repeated.

"Oh my God. Sunnie is going to kill me. I've got the vodka for the punch." Darcy pulled a liquor store bag from her bottom desk drawer.

"You have liquor in your desk?"

She laughed. "I ran out and grabbed it on my lunch break. And it's not like it's in a flask." Then, because she couldn't help herself, she joked, "Just to be clear, a flask in my desk would be frowned upon, right?"

"It would," he deadpanned.

He didn't laugh, but Darcy was used to that and didn't take it to heart. Hell, she took it as a challenge and had for years. On the rare occasions she'd managed to make him chuckle, she honestly felt like she'd won the Olympic gold.

She quickly saved her work and shut down her computer. Then she noticed Ryder had his briefcase.

"You done for the day too?" she asked.

He nodded. "I was just leaving when I saw the light on in here. I'll walk you to your car. It's late."

That sealed it. She was working this late every night for the rest of her life. She smiled, hoping she was managing to project an air of coolness. "Let me guess. You aren't coming to the Halloween party."

Ryder shook his head. "No. I'm not. Long week. I'm tired. Though I appreciate the invitation." His tone didn't suggest he appreciated it at all. Instead, she got the sense he wished she and Yvonne would stop inviting him to stuff so he wouldn't have to keep coming up with excuses.

And while she wasn't surprised he wasn't attending, she was disappointed.

Ryder still shared a house with Leo, and now Yvonne. Leo and Ryder had put an addition on their home to accommodate them all so Vince and Clint, thirteen and eleven, were still together in the same home. Yvonne had just had a baby girl, Reba, a couple of months earlier, so the unconventional yet wonderful family continued to grow.

"You know, you could try to surprise us every once in a while. Rather than being so predictable."

"I prefer consistency."

Yvonne and Darcy had invited Ryder to countless Collins parties over the years, but he always turned them down, claiming he had too much work to do either here at the office or at the house. From what Darcy could see, the man worked twenty-four-seven, his cell phone constantly in his hand. She suspected he probably slept with the damn thing under his pillow at night. And when he wasn't working, he was with the boys.

Ryder had zero social life, a concept that seemed downright foreign to Darcy, who lived for her family's crazy, fun parties.

Tonight was their annual Halloween party, and it kicked off what Darcy referred to as "the social season." The holidays were her absolute favorite time of the year, and the Collins clan did it right. This year, like every year, they were hosting get-togethers for Halloween, Friendsgiving, Thanksgiving, Christmas, and New Year's Eve, either in the family's pub or above it in the Collins Dorm, the apartment Darcy shared with her cousins, Colm and Oliver, as well as Oliver's foster brother, Gavin.

To make the season even crazier, they'd added an extra party, a Boob Voyage party for Darcy's godmother, Bubbles, who was having breast reduction surgery in December.

It was going to be two months of madness starting tonight, and Darcy couldn't wait. She put her coat on, and then grabbed her purse and the vodka.

Ryder waited patiently, looking as hot as ever in his tailor-made black suit and pressed, crisp white dress shirt. Today, he'd at least attempted something whimsical and completely out of character by wearing a black tie with tiny orange jack-o-lanterns on it. In the boring world Ryder chose to exist in, the tie was downright madness, and she loved it.

Darcy silently chastised herself for her never-ending fascination with the man. She was two of the world's worst clichés. The woman who had a crush on her too-hot-for-words boss, as well as the babysitter with a crush on the dad.

Jesus.

Darcy wished she could kick her feelings, but they clearly weren't going anywhere anytime soon. So here she was. The twenty-four-year-old virgin with—*fuck*—a crush on her older boss.

Sadly, Ryder didn't see her as anything more than said employee/babysitter.

To him, she was stuck solely in some sort of limbo land where she was more than an acquaintance, but not quite a friend; someone special not because of *his* feelings toward her, but because of his sons' feelings for her, and a bit more than just an employee because of a longer, more personal association.

Basically, she was a whole lot of nothing.

About the best thing she could say was that he didn't seem to view her as a kid-sister type, because that would have driven her insane. She already had a big brother and too many overprotective male cousins. She didn't need one more of those.

They walked to the elevator side by side, neither of them talking, which was strange for her. Him not talking was actually the norm. Ryder's side of any conversation between the two of them was usually him responding to her questions or comments. He was a quiet, introspective man, and Darcy wondered if that was part of his appeal. She was part of a huge family of boisterous, can't-get-a-word-in-edgewise people—the male relatives as loud and talkative as the women, especially when sports and wagers were the topics.

Ryder seemed to spend a lot of time in his own head, alone with his thoughts, and Darcy was dying to get a glimpse inside. He also projected an air of alpha male that she found super sexy. She'd spent too many nights recalling the way he'd wrapped that belt around his hand the evening he'd come home drunk all those years ago.

Since then, Darcy had become fascinated by the concept of domination and submission. Her cousin Caitlyn had married a Dominant man, and she had probably answered at least a million and twelve of Darcy's questions about their relationship in the past couple of years.

Of course, Ryder wasn't all work and no play. Darcy had caught more than a few glimpses of his playful side with Clint and Vince. The way he teased and joked around with his sons reminded her of her close relationship with her own dad, Aaron.

However, it was safe to say that most of the time, and with the exception of the boys, Ryder was serious and reserved, a sexy mystery, which simply ensured he kept Darcy captivated.

Ryder didn't glance her direction as they stepped onto the elevator. Instead, he pushed the button to the bottom floor and waited as the doors closed.

The man was completely oblivious to her feelings for him. Which she could admit was her own fault. After all, she worked overtime to act completely natural around him, though she knew her family suspected her feelings.

It was hard enough to know her crush was one-sided, so there was no way she'd make a jackass of herself mooning over him or making him uncomfortable with unrequited feelings.

They'd only descended a few floors when the lights flickered. The elevator stopped rather abruptly, and Darcy had to quickly reach out to the side wall to steady herself. The lights went out completely for a second or two before emergency backup lights flashed on. They were much dimmer than the real lights—more pale gold than bright, fluorescent white.

Darcy took a deep, steadying breath and closed her eyes. "Please start moving again," she whispered. Their offices occupied the entire fifteenth floor of one of Baltimore's tallest skyscrapers. If she had to guess, she'd say they hadn't passed the tenth floor yet.

Ryder sighed. "Dammit."

"No." Darcy shook her head. "Not dammit. Don't say dammit."

He turned to look at her and grimaced. "It would appear the power has gone out."

"Can we open the doors?"

Ryder shook his head. "No. I'm fairly certain we can't." He pressed the emergency call button, and Darcy could have cried in relief when a voice responded.

"This is Ryder Hagen. The elevator has stopped."

"I'm sorry, Mr. Hagen. This is Rodney at the security desk. There's a power outage and it appears to have taken down a large chunk of the city. I'm trying to find out now how long they anticipate it will be out."

"Okay. Will you let us know when you find out?" Ryder asked, looking put out, but also at ease, considering their situation.

"Of course, sir," Rodney replied.

"There's no way to get us out of here?" Darcy asked Ryder, hating how breathy her voice sounded. It was as if her throat had closed and she suddenly couldn't get any sound through.

"Is it possible to open these doors manually?" Ryder asked the man on the other end of the call button.

"I'm afraid not, sir. Are you alone?"

Ryder glanced around the elevator. "Isn't there a camera in here, Rodney?"

"Camera is down due to the power outage."

"I see. There's another person trapped as well. Darcy Young."

Darcy swallowed hard, wishing Ryder wouldn't use the word *trapped.*

"Are you both okay?" Rodney asked.

"We're fine."

Darcy wouldn't use the word *fine*, either. Because she was not fine.

"I'm sorry to say I think you'll both have to sit tight at this point. As I said, I'll let you know how long the expected outage time is as soon as I find out."

"Thank you," Ryder said, taking his finger away from the button, then looking at her. "So we're stuck."

Darcy nodded slowly, working overtime to contain the freak-out threatening to erupt.

She must have been successful because Ryder didn't appear to notice her distress. He put down his briefcase, took off his suit jacket, loosened his tie, and leaned against the back wall of the elevator casually. Like he didn't have a care in the world.

Meanwhile, she was struggling not to throw up.

They both stood there, silent for a few minutes, as the reality of the situation sank in. Ryder was taking it in stride, though she knew him well enough to know he was probably more inconvenienced than annoyed.

As for her. Well, she was trembling inside so bad, she didn't know how she wasn't breaking bones.

Darcy jumped when Rodney's voice crackled through the speaker again.

"Mr. Hagen?"

Ryder stepped back to the call button. "Yes."

"I'm afraid I have some bad news."

Darcy shook her head. "No, no bad news," she muttered.

Ryder glanced at her as he spoke to the man. "How long?"

"Looks like several hours. Pretty bad transformer fire in a substation. A lot of the city is currently without power.

Nine-one-one is being bombarded with calls, so I'm not sure I can get anyone here to help you out."

"I understand," he said.

Darcy didn't. She really fucking didn't.

"No firefighters?" she asked Ryder. "Can't they break people out of elevators?"

"You heard him, Darcy. They're fielding a million calls right now," Ryder explained, his finger off the button so the man couldn't hear. "This doesn't exactly constitute an emergency. We aren't in danger or injured."

Darcy and Ryder were going to have to agree to disagree on what constituted an emergency because, in her mind, this was a big one.

Darcy considered calling her dad. Aaron Young was a cop, and he'd hightail it over here to try to get her out if he knew she was stuck. But she couldn't do it. As much as she was freaking out inside, she knew there would be others who would need him more. It wouldn't be right to drag him away from his job just because of what she knew was an irrational fear.

Ryder pressed the button. "We appreciate you letting us know, Rodney."

"I'll be in contact if I'm able to get anyone here to help. Otherwise..."

Ryder went ahead and finished the man's comment when it was obvious he didn't want to point out they were well and truly stuck. "Otherwise, we'll simply wait until the power comes back on."

Ryder returned to his previous spot, leaning against the back wall. She watched as he completely removed his tie and unbuttoned the top button of his shirt. If she weren't struggling for air, Darcy would have found his actions hot. But at the moment, she couldn't get enough oxygen to her brain to appreciate Ryder's sexiness.

Oh God. Was the air thinning out? Were they going to suffocate?

Ryder pointed to the bags she still held. White-knuckled, actually. "Might as well get comfortable, Darcy. It looks like we're going to be in here a few hours."

Hours.

Oh God.

She couldn't do hours!

Then she glanced down and realized... "Vodka."

"Are you proposing we get drunk?"

"It couldn't hurt." In her case, it could only help. She lifted the bag, pulling out a bottle.

She was surprised when Ryder took the bottle of Grey Goose from her and opened it before handing it back.

"Ladies first."

She grinned, lifted it in a silent cheers, and took a drink, wincing slightly. "Oh, what I'd give for some orange juice." Darcy handed it to Ryder, who took a longer swig.

"I'd prefer vermouth and an olive."

"Shaken not stirred, James?" she teased, grateful for the conversation. If she'd been trapped alone, she'd be in the fetal position in the corner already.

"Shhh. My identity is a secret."

"Careful, Ryder. That's dangerously close to a sense of humor." Darcy laughed as he put the cap back on the bottle and set it on the floor between them. She and Yvonne teased him about his general lack of silliness. The man was the epitome of buttoned-up and serious.

"I'll tread lightly," he deadpanned, causing her eyes to widen. Two jokes in a row. This was a record.

Darcy slid down the wall at her back until she was sitting. Ryder followed suit, sighing heavily.

"Not exactly the Halloween you had planned," he said.

She shook her head. "Nope. By now, I would have expected to have put a dent in Sunnie's spiked punch, and everyone would have raved over my Wonder Woman costume."

"I can see you as Wonder Woman," Ryder said. "God knows Clint sees you that way."

Darcy was touched by Ryder's compliment. She was crazy about his son too. "Was Clint doing anything for Halloween?"

"He's spending the night at his best friend Charlie's house. Charlie's mom was planning to take them out trick-or-treating. He's Mario to Charlie's Luigi."

"Clint will rock a Mario costume."

Ryder nodded. "The kid is video game crazy."

"Nothing wrong with that."

Ryder rolled his eyes, though he didn't look annoyed as much as amused. Darcy, Vince, and Clint had spent literally hundreds of hours in the past four years, either online together or whenever she was babysitting or visiting with Yvonne, playing all sorts of video games. They'd gone through a major Mario Kart phase, and they were now obsessed with Fortnite.

Ryder said she was a bad influence on his sons, but she knew he didn't mean it, especially considering the number of times he'd come over to watch them, asking questions about whatever game they were playing, as if he'd like to join in. She'd offered him the controller countless times, but he always shook his head and said he preferred to "leave the gaming to the professionals."

"No Halloween costume for you?" she asked.

"I'm wearing it right now. Haggard businessman stuck in an elevator."

"I guess this is karma trying to teach us both a lesson about working so late on a Friday night."

Ryder shrugged one shoulder. "I work later than this most Fridays."

"Why?"

Ryder frowned. "Why what?"

"Why do you work such long hours? You don't have to. I know you've got plenty of people working for you who would take on more duties if you'd let them."

"I like to work," Ryder said, but given the way he didn't quite look her in the eye, she realized he was lying.

Darcy rested her head back against the wall as she considered that. She'd met Ryder shortly after his wife died, and the first word that popped into her mind whenever she considered how to describe Ryder—after sex-on-a-stick—was workaholic.

Ryder picked up the bottle of vodka and took another drink before offering it to her. She smiled her thanks and drank. Maybe if she was lucky, the alcohol would work its way through her system and help her find a way to relax. As it was, she was very close to having a full-blown panic attack, complete with hyperventilating.

It was bad enough Ryder didn't see her as anything more than Yvonne's younger cousin, the babysitter. The last thing she wanted to do was make an ass of herself by coming completely unhinged in the elevator.

She'd like to capture his attention. But not that way.

As it was, this was the longest the two of them had ever been alone together, if she didn't count the night he'd come home drunk. Which she didn't, because it had been obvious the next time she'd seen him that he didn't remember that conversation at all.

No, their "alone time" was the few minutes when he got home from work when she was watching the boys, and they'd say a couple awkward words, he'd pay her, and she'd drive home.

After putting the boys to bed, she'd always wait with anticipation, hoping Ryder would get home before Leo, then feeling like shit the whole way home, hating that she was so young...and invisible...to the only man who'd ever made her heart race.

"Maybe," she started, trying to figure out some way to distract herself from the fact the walls appeared to be closing in on them. "Maybe we could play a game or something."

Ryder glanced at her. "Like twenty questions?"

She shrugged. "I hate twenty questions. Spin the bottle?" she joked. Well, half-joked. She'd dreamed of kissing Ryder so many times, there was a part of her that now believed they actually had.

God. Pathetic much, Darcy?

"Not much suspense in that. Besides, I'd hate to spill any of the vodka. It sounds like we're going to be in here for a while."

She wished he wouldn't remind her about that. "I'd suggest Truth or Dare, but there aren't a lot of dare options."

"Not appropriate ones."

Darcy quietly drew in a surprised—okay, aroused—breath as she looked in his direction, letting her mind fill in all the inappropriate—alright, kinky—dares she'd like to try with him.

Ryder, as always, was clueless to her reaction. Instead, he glanced at his phone. She suspected if she wasn't here, he'd simply continue to work, answering emails on his phone until the battery died or the power returned.

"What about just the truth part?" she asked.

"Is that a game?" Ryder looked up, and then—she was pleased to notice—he slipped his phone back into his jacket pocket.

"We'll call it a get-to-know-you game."

"We've known each other for four years. You've been in my house about a hundred times."

"And yet, I don't feel like I know you as well as I should."

Ryder studied her face for a moment, and it seemed to Darcy like he was actually just now realizing she was there and might want to talk. She swallowed down the hurt of always being invisible to this man. "I suppose you're right. Okay. How do we start?"

"We can just take turns asking whatever we want to know." Darcy slipped off her shoes, tucking one foot underneath her other leg as she turned toward him. "For example, what do you think is the best movie ever made?"

Ryder didn't even hesitate to respond. "That's easy. *Blade Runner*."

Darcy wrinkled her nose. "Ew."

He quickly added, "The old one with Harrison Ford. Not the new one."

"It doesn't matter."

Ryder scowled. "Of course it does. So what's your answer to that question?"

"*The Princess Bride*."

He closed his eyes and shook his head. "Darcy. That is *not* the best movie ever made."

"You must be crazy. It has everything you could ever want in a movie. Pirates, sword fights, humor, kidnapping, true love, scary creatures, Billy freaking Crystal. Have you ever seen it?"

"You exposed my son to that movie when he was eight years old. I've seen it more times than I care to admit."

Darcy grinned. Vince had been too cool for *The Princess Bride*, but the same did not hold true for Clint. "Clint loved it the first time we watched it."

"I'm aware."

"I want a love like Buttercup and Westley."

"Darcy—" Ryder began, but she cut him off. She'd been around him enough to know he had more than a healthy amount of cynicism, especially when it came to romance and love. Which struck her as odd, considering he'd been married before.

"I mean it. I want someone to love me with that much passion, to be willing to fight to the pain for me. I want to be put up on a pedestal and treated like a princess."

"Nice to know you have such reasonable, achievable goals."

She laughed at his sarcasm. "I'm not asking for something I wouldn't give back in return. When I fall in love, it'll be with my whole heart. I want a relationship like my Pop Pop and Grandma Sunday had. I know *The Princess Bride* is just a movie, but I also know for a fact that kind of relationship can exist in real life. Pop Pop had it. And my parents have it. Leo and Yvonne too."

"I hope you get it," Ryder said, though his tone implied he didn't believe she would. "And for the record, I stand by my choice for greatest movie ever made."

Darcy tilted her head. "Does Clint watch *Blade Runner* with you?"

Ryder held her gaze, then sighed. "No. He typically leaves the room about fifteen minutes in."

Darcy lifted one hand in a "there you go" gesture. "And yet, he'll watch *The Princess Bride* over and over. I rest my case. Your turn to ask a question."

Ryder asked her who her favorite singer was, and mercifully, the time began to pass quickly as they passed the bottle of vodka back and forth, covering every topic from politics to religion to cooking shows.

"Okay," Darcy said, the vodka making her bolder with each passing question. "Who was your first kiss?"

Ryder, who'd rolled up the sleeves on his dress shirt, looked more relaxed than Darcy had ever seen him. Like her, he'd slipped off his shoes, and he leaned back against the elevator wall. He actually seemed...younger. And it occurred to her that, while he was only ten years older than her—thirty-four to her twenty-four—there were times when that age gap felt much vaster. Probably because Ryder had already lived a lifetime—finding success in his career, marrying, raising a son and stepson—while Darcy was still at the beginning of...well...everything.

She'd just gotten her master's degree, landed her first real job, was still single, and living with her cousins in the apartment above the family's pub. Twenty-four years of life and she hadn't gone more than a couple steps toward adulthood. Meanwhile, Ryder gave the appearance of having had enough of adulthood to last him a good long time.

"Third grade," he said. "Brenda Goodman."

Darcy shook her head. "No. First *real* kiss."

"Ah. Well then. That would be Taylor Shipley. Eighth grade. My first girlfriend."

"Was it true love?" Darcy teased.

"No. It had less to do with emotions and more to do with the fact that she let me touch her boobs. When that grew old, I tried to break up with her. Several times. Took quite a few attempts before it would stick."

"Why?"

"Because I was a thirteen-year-old boy and it was easier to say we could keep being boyfriend/girlfriend than listen to her either cry or scream at me."

"Wow. Not very romantic."

Ryder, who'd lifted the bottle of vodka for another sip, put it down. "I'm afraid *The Princess Bride* has given you a fairly skewed view of relationships. The reality of it is, true love doesn't exist."

Darcy sucked in a sharp breath, eyes narrowed. "You don't seriously believe that."

Ryder capped the Grey Goose without taking a drink and leaned forward. "With every fiber of my being."

Darcy didn't know how to respond to that because there was no doubt in her mind he meant what he said.

"What about *your* first kiss?" Ryder asked.

"I was older. Tenth grade, after a home football game. The boy I liked, Trey Nichols, tugged me away from our group of friends and asked if I wanted to go to Homecoming with him. When I said yes, he gave me a kiss. It was just a quick one, no tongue," she added. "I'm pretty sure it was his first kiss too."

"No fireworks, no sword fighting, no proclamation of undying true love?"

Darcy narrowed her eyes. "I know you're teasing me. But no. Not that time."

"*That* time?"

"Actually," Darcy blew out a long breath, "not any time. Yet," she quickly added.

"Yeah well, heads up. I'm thirty-four and I haven't gotten there yet, either."

Darcy fell silent, especially when it was clear Ryder hadn't meant to reveal so much about himself. This time when he picked up the vodka, he took a long drink, and she realized they'd put a pretty serious dent in the bottle. She had a million follow-up questions she wanted to ask about that revelation, but something about the sudden stiffness in his shoulders told her he wouldn't answer them.

He'd been married, yet he claimed he'd never felt true love.

"Your turn," she prodded, terrified he'd want to call a halt to the game when he glanced at his phone again, and she got the sense he was trying to pull away. The vodka and the distraction had helped her. If he decided he didn't want to talk anymore, she'd have way too much time to remember...

Fuck.

Where they were.

She swallowed down the panic rising in her chest. She

read the time on his phone. It was nearly eleven. They'd been stuck in the elevator almost two hours.

"Why did you choose to pursue a career in graphic arts?" Ryder asked at last, tucking the phone away again, and Darcy released a sigh of relief. They spent the next few minutes discussing their chosen majors in college, and she was able to beat down the fear once more.

Darcy took another sip of vodka. She'd drunk enough that she was going to have to call a rideshare to get home.

Then she considered her next question. There were countless things she wanted to ask, her curiosity piqued by his earlier comment about love, but she was more terrified of him calling the game to a halt if she asked something he wasn't comfortable with. "What's your ideal date?" she asked instead, playing it safe.

"I don't date."

Darcy thought back over the past four years and all the babysitting she'd done for him. Every single time Ryder had asked her to keep an eye on the boys, it was because he was working late.

"Ever?"

Ryder shook his head. "Work and the boys keep me too busy for dating."

"That's not true." The words flew out before she could stop them.

Mercifully, Ryder didn't take offense. "You're right. It's not true. I choose not to date."

"Why?"

Ryder rubbed his eyes wearily. "I find most women date with marriage in mind. I'm not getting married again."

"Ever?" Darcy tried to ignore the sudden pang in her

heart when she realized Ryder definitely meant what he said.

"Ever. My life is uncomplicated. I like it that way."

It wasn't much of an answer, but then Darcy realized it was probably the truth and as much as she was going to get. Especially when Ryder turned the question around to her.

"And your ideal date?" he asked. "Roses? Candlelight? Soft music?"

She laughed. "You read me like a book. And yes, all that. I want to be picked up in a limousine."

Ryder snorted. "A limo? Seriously?"

"It's my ideal date, Ryder. I can have a limo if I want. Besides, I've never ridden in one and I've always wanted to."

"You've never been in a limo? Not for prom or a wedding?"

Darcy shook her head. "Nope. Never. And I'm dying to."

"So this dream guy—we'll call him Westley—comes to pick you up in a limo. Then what?"

"We'll drink champagne and tell the driver to put up the blackout screen so we can make out."

"At the beginning of the date? Very nice."

Darcy giggled, realizing the vodka was working its magic on both of them. She reached over and punched him on the arm playfully. "Anyway, he'll take me back to his place for dinner. And it'll be just like you said. Candlelight and roses, soft music. All through the meal, we'll talk about our hopes and dreams for the future, then after dinner, we'll dance in his living room and then..."

"Sex." Ryder filled in the blank with just one word, and Darcy frowned, shaking her head.

"No. Not just sex. That's the least imaginative way to describe it."

"I suppose you prefer *making love?*"

His words didn't bug Darcy as much as his tone. Because he'd never made it more clear he didn't see her as a woman, but as the too-young babysitter who immaturely viewed the world through *Princess Bride*, rose-colored glasses.

Darcy considered all the things her sister, Sunnie, and her cousins, Caitlyn and Yvonne, had shared about their sex lives over the years. They were all close and there were very few—if any—secrets between them. As such, Darcy had acquired plenty of sex details to fuel her masturbation fantasies. "I want what Yvonne and Leo have in the bedroom. Apparently, Leo—"

Ryder raised one hand. "Please. I'd prefer not to know exactly what those two are doing in the room down the hall."

"You can't hear it?" she joked.

"Darcy," he said, lacing his tone with a warning. "Maybe we should just leave this conversation here."

Darcy had played it cool with Ryder for years, pushed her feelings for the man deep, deep down because the truth was, when they'd first met, his wife had just died and she *had* been too young for him. She'd only been twenty and not even able to legally drink.

But now...well...now she was older. And she was ready to open his eyes to that fact.

"No, I don't want to leave it here." Darcy took a deep breath. "What I want is something better than just sex or making love. I want raw, rough, earth-shattering, break-the-bed passion. I want to be held down, tied up, spanked, and fucked hard by a man who knows what he wants—and what he wants is *me*. Just me. However he can get me. And then I want soft, gentle, peaceful-as-a-boat-on-a-placid-lake sex. With kisses and sweet words. I want it all. With the man I love, who loves me back."

"Jesus," Ryder muttered under his breath, his eyes dark with something Darcy couldn't recognize.

She grinned to herself, aware she'd finally done it.

Ryder was looking at her.

And for the first time ever...he was *seeing* her.

CHAPTER THREE

Ryder lifted one of his legs, casually draping his arm over his knee. Not because it was a more comfortable position, but because he needed to hide the evidence of the impact Darcy's words had on him.

His cock was on full alert, thick, rock hard. Something he was struggling to believe.

No woman had managed that feat since...

Ryder closed his eyes, refusing to think her name. Then he tried to will away his hard-on, to find a way to fight down this sudden and unexpected arousal. He counted to ten, then to twenty, then he started to recite the alphabet...in Greek.

Unfortunately, nothing worked.

"And that," Darcy said after a few quiet moments, her voice light and breezy, as if she hadn't just dropped a big fucking bomb in the middle of the elevator, "is my ideal date."

"That's..." Ryder cleared his throat, digging deep for a

tone, for words that wouldn't give away his current state. "That's quite a date."

Darcy laughed lightly. "Your turn to ask a question."

Ryder shook his head. There wasn't enough blood pumping to his brain to allow him to come up with a single question.

Instead, he was too busy imagining taking Darcy in all the ways she'd just described.

Darcy, for God's sake.

There was no way he should even be entertaining the thought. She was certainly one of those women who dated with marriage in mind. Besides, she was too young for him, too bubbly and happy and sweet and...

Innocent was the next word that flashed in his mind... before he recalled her ideal date. Darcy obviously had a wild side, something he wouldn't have foreseen. Not that he'd ever considered anything even remotely sexual in terms of Darcy.

"I can't think of any more questions," he admitted.

Darcy bit her lower lip as something he couldn't recognize flashed across her face. For a second, he thought she looked almost scared. Was she afraid she'd gone too far? Revealed too much? After all, he was her boss.

"Darcy, I know we didn't...nothing that's said tonight leaves here. This is Vegas. You don't have to worry—"

"Oh, I'm not worried about that," she interjected before he could finish offering his reassurances that anything she'd said would impact her job. "I trust you completely."

"Good," he said, still curious about the fear he'd just seen. Darcy didn't give him time to worry about it.

"Lucky for you," she said with an adorable smile. "I still have plenty of questions to keep the game going."

Adorable smile?

Since when did he notice Darcy's smile? Or her bright, expressive blue eyes? Or her long, thick, wavy, dark hair that smelled like coconut?

Dammit. This wasn't good.

He recalled the first time he'd met Darcy. It was right after Denise had died. He and Leo had been working on the memorial together and they'd needed to go to the funeral home. They'd wanted Yvonne to go with them to help them with the arrangements, but they hadn't wanted to take the boys. Yvonne had shown up with Darcy in tow, introducing her as her "baby cousin," a term Ryder had since come to learn the older Collins' cousins used for Darcy and Oliver, the youngest two in her large family.

Darcy had only been twenty, a fresh-faced college junior at a local university. She'd shown up in denim overalls, with a hot pink tank top beneath, and her hair in long braids on either side of her head. She'd bounced into the house, a bundle of energy armed with a new video game, and for the first time since losing their mother, Vince and Clint had actually smiled.

She'd been back to the house countless times since then, and she'd solidified her place in his son's heart. Clint talked about Darcy like she hung the moon.

She—and Yvonne—had come into Ryder's life when he was at his lowest point, the world around him so dark, he couldn't see his own hand in front of his face. She'd stepped in time after time to help in the past four years, always available, even at short notice. And he didn't question for a second that she loved his sons every bit as much as they loved her.

It was one of the reasons he'd gone to bat to help her get a job with the marketing department. He knew she had a can-do attitude and a good work ethic, something she'd proven in her short time working here. Helen had thanked him earlier in the week for recommending her.

Regardless of all that, Ryder wasn't sure he'd ever really noticed, really seen Darcy as anything more than that young, hardworking girl in the overalls who'd become an important person—a much-needed female influence—in his sons' lives. Before tonight.

"Not sure how you could top that last question," he said, trying once more to put them back on steady footing. The last thing he needed to do was start to think of Darcy as... Jesus...a sexy woman.

One with desires that had just awakened something long dead inside him.

Darcy winked. "You ain't seen nothing yet."

"Should I be frightened?"

She smacked his forearm lightly, and he realized she always touched him like that. Playful taps and jabs and hip bumps, like they were two kids in middle school.

He'd been a standoffish asshole for years. So much so, most people gave him a wide berth. And apart from rough-housing with the boys or hugging them good night, *no one* touched him. It hadn't occurred to him until now that Darcy was the only other person who didn't shy away from touching him physically. She never had.

"I'll take it easy on you," she promised. "Tell me a secret about yourself. Something no one else knows."

"A secret," he repeated slowly.

Ryder felt his spine stiffen, his blood suddenly going cold. It was an innocuous enough request. And he could make up anything, tell her anything, and they could move on.

But he only had one secret. One thing that had been eating away at his soul, bit by bit for the past four years.

Darcy seemed oblivious to his current unease. "Something scandalous," she joked. "You snore like a chainsaw or you do cosplay or you play the bagpipes in a kilt with nothing underneath it."

"I don't snore, I don't dress up, and I play no instruments."

Darcy glanced at him curiously. Even to his own ears, his words sounded wooden.

"I notice you didn't mention whether or not you go commando."

The Ryder he'd been a lifetime ago might have laughed at that, but he couldn't right now. Not because she wasn't funny, but because her question was still rolling around in his brain like a grenade set to explode.

Silence fell between them, and it hovered for too long.

He assumed Darcy was giving him time to think of a secret, but when the minutes dragged on, she finally noticed his distress.

And, because it was Darcy, who had a kind heart, she tried to let him off the hook. "It's a silly question," she said. "I'll think of another."

"No." The single word came out louder than he'd intended, startling Darcy, who jerked slightly. "No. I want to answer it."

Darcy nodded but said nothing more.

He lifted the bottle of vodka and took a long pull, trying to figure out if he was really going to do this. Going to tell her.

"I've never...told anyone..."

"You don't have to tell me if you don't want to," she said, once again giving him an out.

Ryder had sworn to himself he'd never share this secret with another living soul. But suddenly, he *wanted* to tell Darcy. He'd revealed more of himself to her in the last two and a half hours than he had with anyone in his entire life. And it bothered him to realize that. He'd blamed Denise's death for so many things. For the way he didn't open up to others or let people in. The way he held the people closest to him at arm's length.

Now, he could see he'd always been a distant bastard, more at ease with casual acquaintances, less comfortable with making a close friend.

He'd had a million buddies in high school and college, but none he would consider a true friend—proven by the fact he hadn't bothered to stay in touch with a single one of them. Leo was probably the closest he had to a real friend, and even with him, Ryder held huge pieces of himself back.

"The day Denise died..." he began.

Darcy's eyes widened, and he knew he'd shocked her. His wife's death was something he never, *ever* talked about. Darcy would know that—no doubt told by Yvonne and Leo, and probably even Clint.

"The day she died, I had an early meeting at work. Typically, I was still home when she left to take the boys to school, but that day, I left first. She was in the kitchen making them breakfast, packing their lunches. I called out goodbye from the front door and left."

Darcy nodded slowly. "You regret not kissing her goodbye?" she asked softly.

Ryder huffed out a harsh breath, a cross between an unamused laugh and snort. Of course, the queen of romance *would* think that was what was bothering him. Guilt over a forgotten goodbye kiss.

He shook his head. "We never kissed goodbye, Darcy."

"Oh." She managed to pack a lot of sadness into that single syllable, and it opened Ryder's eyes to so many—too many—things about his marriage. Things he'd chosen not to see, chosen to bury under a mountain of anger.

"Around lunchtime, two police officers showed up at my office. They told me Denise had been killed in a car accident. She'd run a stop sign and been sideswiped by a truck. The officers said she hadn't suffered, that she'd been killed instantly."

"That couldn't have been easy to hear."

"Numbness set in the second they said she was gone."

"You were probably in shock."

Ryder nodded once, acknowledging that. "I went to the hospital to identify her body and they gave me her personal belongings. Her wedding ring, a necklace, her purse. I called Denise's parents from the hospital parking lot—they'd moved to St. Louis after her dad was transferred for work— and then I called Leo and met him at your family's pub to tell him."

He and Leo hadn't been friends at the time. Hell, they'd barely been acquaintances, even though Ryder was Vince's stepdad. Ryder was estranged from his parents. And he wasn't close to any of his work colleagues, so he hadn't had anyone else to turn to.

"I can't imagine how hard all of that must have been," Darcy said.

"The hardest part was telling Clint and Vince. Leo was there with me. He actually said the words. I couldn't. Vince wanted his dad with him, so Leo spent the night. He and Vince shared the boys' room, and I took Clint to my bedroom, held him until he cried himself to sleep in my bed."

"No little boy should lose his mom at seven years old."

Ryder agreed with that, but he couldn't say it, couldn't even nod. Because his throat was too tight. It was as if his body was rejecting telling the rest of the story.

The secret.

"I got up to..." Ryder tried to take a breath, but it was hard to get air to his lungs.

Darcy must have noticed because she shifted closer, moving until she was sitting right next to him rather than across the elevator. She reached over and took his hand. He squeezed it, taking comfort from it.

"I got up to get ready for bed and I saw...an envelope on the dresser with my name on it. In Denise's handwriting."

Darcy turned toward him, her eyes locked on his profile, still holding his hand.

"She'd left me a letter."

Darcy's brows lowered in confusion. "I don't understand."

"She was leaving me. In the letter, she said she'd met someone else. She'd been having an affair, and she wanted a divorce. I looked around the room then...and realized a lot of her stuff was missing."

"Oh my God."

"Her car had been totaled, towed to a garage. A mechanic called a week or so after the accident. Said he'd take care of disposing of the vehicle, but that someone would need to come retrieve the luggage they'd found in the trunk."

"Ryder," Darcy whispered, a tear rolling along her cheek.

He felt the slightest trembling in her hand, so he tightened his grip, grateful to have something to hold on to and touched by her compassion.

"I hired a private investigator a few months after her death to find out who the other man was. I kept telling myself I didn't give a shit, but I couldn't let it go, couldn't stop thinking..."

"Did you find out?"

Ryder nodded. "I did. I thought as soon as I had the name, I'd confront the guy, but...once I knew, I realized I didn't care anymore. It didn't—it wouldn't—change anything. I've never mentioned it to him, but I can tell from the way he looks at me...he knows that I know."

"You see the guy?"

"Unfortunately, due to certain circumstances, we run into each other on occasion."

"Ryder. I don't know what to say. I'm so sorry."

He lifted one shoulder. There really wasn't anything to say. It was the one reason he'd always sworn never to talk about it. There was nothing anyone could do or say to take away the anger or the hurt.

"It's okay," he said, both of them knowing those words were a lie.

That was why he wasn't getting married again. He'd long

ago accepted that he simply didn't have the strength to risk his heart or his pride again.

As the saying went, been there, done that, burned the T-shirt.

They sat there, holding hands, staring at the opposite wall of the elevator, neither of them speaking for several minutes. Through his peripheral vision, he caught sight of her trying to covertly wipe her eyes a couple of times.

He appreciated her tears, even as he marveled he'd never managed to shed a single one. Not for Denise, not for himself, not even for his poor sons. Every drop of sadness had evaporated in the red-hot rage that had coursed through him for years.

"Thank you for telling me."

Ryder turned to face her. He couldn't begin to understand what had prompted him to open up to her, but he didn't regret it. Perhaps that was the most surprising part. And in some strange way, he actually felt lighter, like the burden of that secret was no longer only his to carry.

But now...he needed to forget again. "Your turn."

She tilted her head, confused. "What?"

"A secret."

She smiled, though the expression was wobbly at best. "Oh. That's easy. I'm extremely claustrophobic."

Ryder scowled, recalling the brief flashes of fear he'd seen in her face over the past few hours. "Darcy—" he started.

"Yep," she said, drawing his attention to how pale she was. "I've been silently screaming inside my head since the power went out."

Ryder reached out for her, tugging her into his embrace. "I didn't know."

"That's what made it a secret." She was reaching for levity, trying to mask her feelings with lighthearted words. They were both guilty of trying to shield their true feelings through jokes and casual comments tonight.

He held her tightly, trying not to acknowledge how good she felt in his arms. It was the first time he'd hugged her, and as he held her, he realized he wanted more than just a friendly embrace.

Fuck. He wanted way more.

"Are you okay?" he asked, forcing himself to release her.

"As long as I don't think about it too much." Her eyes traveled around the elevator, and he heard her take in a shaky breath.

"You're thinking about it."

She closed her eyes tightly, once again appearing to struggle to breathe. "The game was helping me forget."

Ryder placed his hands on her cheeks. "Look at me, Darcy."

She slowly opened her beautiful blue eyes. They were framed by long, thick lashes.

"Focus on your breathing. Watch me." He took in a deep breath and held it for a few seconds before releasing it. "Do it with me."

Darcy followed his lead, the two of them taking several long, deep breaths.

"In. And out. In. And out," he coached.

"I don't know how much longer I can stand to be in here," she confessed.

"I'm right here. You're going to be fine. I promise. Want more vodka?"

She grinned and shook her head. "No. I'm going to have to take a cab home as it is."

Ryder agreed. "Yeah. Me too. We'll split one. I want to make sure you get home okay. Considering it's a city-wide blackout in Baltimore on Halloween, the truth of the matter is, we're probably both safer in here."

Darcy giggled. "That's a good point. God only knows what my poor dad has had to deal with tonight."

She could have called her father. Ryder knew Aaron Young well enough to know he would have made his daughter his top priority. She didn't. Instead, she rode it out, put on a brave face.

She was incredible.

He still held her face in his hands. He should drop them, should let go.

But...he couldn't.

To make matters worse, Darcy didn't seem to mind the touch. Her hands rested lightly on his wrists, and he got the sense she was trying to hold them in place.

She took in another deep breath, drawing his gaze to her lips. Her full, pink, soft lips. Her tongue darted out to lick the lower one, and Ryder couldn't resist what he recognized as an invitation.

"Darcy," he murmured softly.

"Yes?" she whispered.

"This has to stay here too."

She frowned, confused, until he leaned forward and placed his lips on hers, kissing her.

He'd expected her to be shocked, to perhaps pull away... but Darcy did neither of those things.

Instead, she tilted her head, parted her lips, and allowed him to deepen the kiss, their tongues touching. He tasted the vodka they'd shared, felt the heat from her breath.

Her hands left his wrists, moving to rest on his shoulders, while he retained his grip on her face, capturing her low moan, the sound one of pure desire. Before he knew it, he was moaning as well, hungry for more.

Ryder felt as if he could devour her completely and still not have his fill.

It was a kiss.

Just a kiss.

Yet, it was so much more.

For several long, heated minutes, they explored each other's mouths, tasted, touched, took.

Ryder had kissed countless women in his past, but it had never affected him like this.

Perhaps it was because it had been so long since he'd held a woman. Or because he'd sworn women off entirely, never expecting to kiss someone like this again.

Or because it was Darcy.

He dismissed that last thought immediately.

This couldn't—shouldn't—be happening.

"Darcy. We have to stop," he breathed against her cheek, dragging his lips along the soft skin of her face to her ear. He'd released her lips, intent on pulling away, but he hadn't managed to move an inch away before he was back, seeking, taking more.

"Don't stop." Darcy's arm tightened around his neck,

using her own mouth to explore him, placing kisses on his cheek, his neck.

Don't stop.

Her words niggled at the back of his brain. A foggy memory? A dream?

An image of Darcy unbuttoning his shirt flashed in his mind. Of him saying, "Don't stop."

It never happened, so he pushed the thought aside and bit her earlobe, producing the cutest little squeak from her before he licked away the tiny spark of pain. He kept playing her words over and over in his brain.

Tied up. Held down. Spanked. Taken.

Ryder hadn't been with a woman since Denise died. He'd genuinely believed her betrayal had killed that part of him. Because the honest-to-God truth was, he hadn't had a hard-on in four years. Not once.

About two years after Denise's death, a woman he knew through mutual acquaintances began making advances, letting him know in no uncertain terms she was interested in a casual affair. Ryder had thought the offer ideal. Sex with no strings, no emotions, no commitment.

They'd decided to meet at a hotel. However, it soon became evident that his heart and his dick weren't into it. He'd made a lame excuse to leave, said an awkward goodbye, and never saw her again.

After that, he'd tried to discover if his problem had just been a lack of attraction to the woman, but countless experiments had proven the problem was his. He'd watched hours and hours of porn. Gone to a strip club for a work colleague's bachelor party. Read erotica. His body responded to none of it.

And he'd found another reason for rage.

Impotence.

Or so he'd thought.

"Darcy," he whispered when she pulled the hem of his dress shirt from his pants, her hands slipping beneath to touch his bare chest.

His dick had never been this hard, this thick. It was pulsing, aching. He was two minutes away from pushing Darcy to the floor of this elevator, pulling up her skirt, and pounding his way inside her.

Ryder fought for control, but Darcy kept stripping it away, piece by piece. She ran her fingernails over his chest, tangling her fingers in the light smattering of hair there, then she let them drift lower.

He gripped her wrists, pulling her hands away just before she could cup his dick through his dress pants.

"Bad girl," he murmured, wishing his words hadn't put such a sexy, wicked grin on her face.

Too much vodka.

It had to be the alcohol.

Ryder tried to reconcile what was happening, searching for an excuse that made sense. Because he didn't act out of character.

Ever.

And this...this man wasn't him.

Not even close.

Ryder ignored the tiny voice that said it might not *be* him, but damn if it wasn't *who* he wanted to be.

"I wanna be bad. Very bad," Darcy whispered. "With you."

"Fuck." And then, because he was weak and completely

out of control, he kissed her again, though there was no soft-ness behind it. It was a hard, rough, brutal kiss that was likely to leave bruises.

Ryder twisted her away from the wall at her back and pressed her to the floor, coming over her, his lips never leaving hers.

He caged her beneath him, his weight held only by his elbows as the rest of their bodies were connected everywhere.

Darcy opened her legs, and he accepted her silent invitation, grinding his covered cock against her center.

She gasped, then groaned, her eyes drifting closed as she lifted her hips, searching for more.

He thrust downward again, his own eyes shut as he lost himself in the sensations of mimicking sex.

Sex with Darcy.

His eyes flew open, and once again, he felt that brief determination to pull away. Until he saw her gaze on his face and felt her fingers working to free the buttons of his shirt.

"I want to see you," she said. "Want to lick every part of you."

Mother. Fucker.

Four years was a long goddamned time. Ryder had been far from a saint in his younger years, and shades of his former self reemerged, parts he'd thought he had outgrown or managed to snuff out.

Darcy, with her sweet smile and unending questions, had dragged more than just a long-buried secret from him.

She'd reached even deeper and unleashed a beast.

Her gaze drifted lower once she'd unbuttoned his shirt, studying what she'd unwrapped. He hissed when she drew a single fingernail down the center of his chest, not stopping until she reached the buckle of his belt.

Once again, he got a sense of familiarity...like they'd done this before.

Ryder pushed himself away from her, kneeling between her outstretched legs.

Darcy frowned at the sudden loss of his weight on top of her, and she started to complain.

"No," he said, his tone harsher, harder than normal. "Sit up, Darcy. Take off your shirt and bra."

Her cheeks, which had already been flushed pink from her arousal, deepened to a dark red. His first thought was that she was embarrassed, but that was washed away when Darcy did exactly as he asked, sitting in front of him as she tugged her lightweight sweater over her head in one confident pull.

Her bra was dark blue and lacy, one of those push-up types that showed off a woman's cleavage. Somehow even more blood managed to make its way to his already rock-hard dick.

Darcy looked at him, her eyes betraying a sudden shyness he hadn't felt from her before now.

It didn't help. If anything...it provoked the alpha male inside, the one who needed to be obeyed.

"Take off your bra," he said again.

She reached behind her back, unsnapping her bra. Then, once again, with the confidence of a woman who knew her worth, she slipped the straps off her shoulders and pulled the lace away.

Ryder was a tit man—and Darcy's were fucking perfect. Full, firm, with light pink areolas and large, tight nipples.

One second, he was looking, the next, he was holding them. Ryder cupped her breasts in his large palms, loving the way she filled his hands. Then he lowered his mouth and sucked one of her nipples into his mouth. Hard.

Darcy gasped, her hands flying to his hair.

He increased the suction, expecting her to push him away.

Again, she surprised him, pulling him closer as she threw her head back. "More. God, harder."

He shifted his head, taking her other nipple between his lips—and teeth—as he pinched the one he'd just released, hot and wet from his mouth. Darcy held him close, filling the silence in the elevator with gasps and sighs and quiet moans.

Ryder could have played with her tits all night and never —*never*—gotten tired of it.

"Ryder," Darcy said at last. "I need...God..."

He lifted his head and took in her glazed, unfocused eyes. She was on the verge of coming and he'd yet to touch her below the waist.

Flipping her sweater out, he put it down like a blanket, guiding her to her back on top of it.

Ryder lifted her skirt, grinning when Darcy lifted her hips so he could pull her panties down. He slipped them off.

God help them if the power came back on now.

He was slightly surprised when Darcy—who was clearly all in—tried to close her legs. He pressed them apart with his hands on her thighs.

"Let me look at you."

She blushed even more, something he hadn't thought possible.

"You're beautiful," he whispered, just before he lowered his head and ran his tongue along her slit.

It had been so long since he'd tasted a woman, felt the heat from a woman's pussy. Darcy was soaking wet. He'd noticed that the second he'd pulled down her damp panties.

Ryder used to love sex, used to love being with women. He'd had a reputation in high school and college as being a player, a playboy. A past girlfriend had called him a bad boy, even though he'd rolled his eyes and dismissed the words out of hand. Her comment had been fueled by his sexual tastes, his desire for dominance, for rough sex.

His younger self had actually enjoyed the nicknames, considered them a badge of honor, and he'd cut a swath through cheerleaders and sorority girls. He was more than capable of giving Darcy everything she wanted from a man in the bedroom because he was experienced in all of it—bondage, spankings, control. It was as if her words had been pulled from the Ryder Hagen sex manual.

Or at least, the Ryder Hagen he'd been before marriage.

"Ryder. Oh God," Darcy breathed, lifting her hips toward his mouth. He stroked her with his tongue once more, then turned his attention to her clit.

Darcy started to writhe beneath him, tossing her head from side to side, drawing his attention to her long, dark, oh-so-pullable hair.

He wasn't sure how he'd failed to notice all of this before.

Darcy was the most beautiful woman he'd ever seen.

"More," she demanded again. "Please."

Ryder stroked her clit with his thumb, increasing the speed, the friction. She was close. And he knew exactly how to push her over the edge.

He pushed three fingers inside her, deep, hard.

"Ah!" Darcy gasped loudly, the sound a mix of pleasure and...pain? He lifted his gaze in time to see her slight wince, then her inner muscles clenched against his fingers, and she cried out again, her climax rumbling through her roughly.

One thrust.

God. She'd come with just one thrust of his fingers. He stilled inside her as she rode out her orgasm, trying not to think of how incredible it would be to feel her climax on his dick. She was so tight...so...

He pulled his fingers out slowly, listening to her shaky breath.

"Wow," she said, her tone wholly Darcy. "That was..."

Suddenly, it wasn't just Darcy he was noticing.

It was...more than that.

Way more.

He'd spent the last four years around this woman, never seeing what was now so blindingly bright, in focus, crystal clear.

"Darcy...are you a virgin?"

She bit her lower lip. "Not intentionally."

The answer was so her that he barked out a brief laugh. Even as his chest tightened.

The sound took her by surprise, and even he could hear how rusty it was. He didn't laugh much. "Maybe that was another secret you should have shared."

She sat up gingerly, her gaze drifting lower, checking out what was beneath his belt. There was no way he could hide his erection from her, so he didn't even bother to try.

"Do we have to stop?" she asked.

"Yes." It was one word, the hardest one he'd ever spoken

in his life. But he knew it was for the best, knew he didn't have a choice. Because he couldn't give Darcy what she wanted...and he didn't mean sexually. "I'm not taking your virginity, Darcy. Not on the floor of an elevator. Not anywhere."

"Ryder. I swear I'm not saving myself for marriage or anything like that. I've just never really been with a man I wanted to..."

Her words faded away before she revealed what she didn't want him to know. What he suspected she'd been carefully concealing from him for years behind her breezy, easy, casual attitude.

It didn't matter. Because that was the biggest reveal, the one thing he suddenly saw that he couldn't deny or ignore.

Darcy Young was looking at him like he was her Westley.

And that was someone he wasn't.

CHAPTER FOUR

Darcy was torn between throwing her sweater back on—she suddenly felt very exposed—or throwing herself on top of Ryder and forcing him to finish what they'd started.

She meant what she'd said. She hadn't purposely tried to hold on to her virginity. It was just that she'd had the very good—or bad, or she didn't know what the fuck kind of—luck, meeting Ryder Hagen when she was just barely twenty years old.

After that, every man—boy, really—couldn't hold a candle to him. None of them were virgin-worthy. Not a single one.

Ryder took the choice of getting dressed away from her when he reached down and picked up her bra. She was surprised by how adept and steady he was as he pulled the straps over her arms, tucked her breasts back into the cups, and reached around her to fasten the hooks.

It was totally hot and completely disappointing all at the

same time. She'd confessed that her first date would include a man who would take control, and damn if Ryder hadn't proven himself to be one-hundred percent the man of her dreams in that regard.

Oh hell, who was she fooling?

He was her perfect type straight across the board.

"Ryder," she started again, desperate to change his mind. They'd come so far tonight, and she couldn't stand the thought of losing any ground.

"No, Darcy. This is over. That's nonnegotiable."

"Why?"

He gave her an amused look. "Do you have to question everything?"

She nodded. "Yeah. I do."

She half-expected her response to annoy him, but instead he dismissed it with a soft chuckle. Then he reached behind her, picked up her sweater, and pulled it back on too, dressing her like she was some helpless little girl.

Her temper tweaked at the thought.

"I'm perfectly capable of dressing myself," she grumbled, hating that she sounded a bit like a petulant child.

"I'm aware of that." Even so, he stood up, then reached down to help her. She took his hand instinctively before remembering she was pissed off, allowing him to help her rise as well.

Kneeling, he pulled her panties back up as her skirt fell once more, covering her completely.

Within seconds, he had her dressed again. And despite her anger, his actions had only added kerosene to the fire still raging inside her. It was as if her earlier orgasm had never happened.

She needed him with a desire that physically hurt.

Once he finished setting her to rights, he tackled the buttons on his own shirt, tucking it back in, as she tried to figure out how they could have moved from her coming on his fingers so hard she thought she'd explode to this fully-dressed silence so quickly.

"Ryder," she started. "I think—"

He shook his head, halting her words with just that gesture. Then, suddenly, he was pulling her into his arms, wrapping her up in a hug that was comforting and insulting.

Only Ryder could constantly provoke completely opposite reactions at the same time. His gentleness touched her, set her at ease, even as she felt him trying to pull away from her emotionally.

"Darcy. I let this go way too far."

He did?

He wasn't the only one in the elevator. There were two consenting adults...

Oh, that's right. He still viewed her as a kid, the fucking babysitter.

"I don't think it went far enough," she retorted.

"I'm your boss."

She rolled her eyes so hard, it actually hurt. "Oh, so that's how we're playing this, huh?"

He scowled. "I'm not sure what you mean by that, but—"

"I mean this wasn't some random, stuck-in-an-elevator, vodka-induced hookup. And you know it. We're not strangers, Ryder. Tonight, we shared—"

"More than we should have. And you're wrong. Vodka did play a part. For both of us. We allowed it to lower our inhibitions and we did things we sho—"

"Don't." Her back stiffened as she stared him down, glared at him, dared him with her eyes to finish that sentence, to call what they'd just done a mistake. Because erection or not, she'd knee him in the balls if he did.

Ryder wisely closed his mouth and grimaced.

And Darcy fought to school her features, to hide her grin.

Because she had him now.

He wouldn't say the words because he knew they weren't true.

"And you're not my boss. Helen is."

"I'm Helen's boss, so that makes me your boss."

Darcy considered that. "She gives me my assignments, does my employment evaluations, oversees my work. You don't do any of that. I don't answer to you directly for anything. I'm under Helen's umbrella. A lot lower down on the food chain. So I don't see how work impacts this."

"You're tenacious."

She smiled, taking his words as a compliment, even though she knew he didn't mean them that way. "I'm a Collins. And if you think *I'm* tenacious, you should meet my mother."

"I've met Riley, so I'm perfectly aware of where you get that particular personality trait. Sit down, Darcy," he said, pointing to the floor. Before she could do so, he dropped down first, assuming the same spot he'd occupied for the past few hours.

She followed suit, curious.

"I'm going to tell you another secret."

She nodded, uncertain if this was something she wanted to hear. His first secret had broken her heart, shattered it. She now understood why he was so cynical when it came to romance, but it also made her that much more determined to prove him wrong. To show him that true love did exist.

"I haven't been with a woman since Denise died."

Her eyes widened in surprise, even though she wasn't sure why his secret was that shocking. She knew he didn't date, knew he'd wrapped his life around work and his sons. But even so, fucking wasn't the same thing as dating. And Ryder didn't strike her as the type of man who would do without for so long.

"Why not?"

And she knew the second the words left her mouth, that was one secret Ryder would not reveal to her. She could see it in the tightness around his mouth and the crease in his brow.

Then, he softened his voice. "Darcy, please. You have to let me do the right thing here."

Before she could respond, the lights flickered on and, another moment later, the elevator started to descend.

Darcy and Ryder both slipped their shoes back on, rising and gathering their stuff.

Rodney, the security guard, was waiting on the ground floor when the doors opened, smiling tentatively. "Everyone okay?" he asked.

Darcy nodded, letting Ryder answer the man and thank him for his help. She opened up the rideshare app on her phone, requesting a car for them.

Ryder stepped up next to her. "Is there a very long wait?"

She shook her head. "Nope. Only a minute or two."

"I'm sorry," he murmured quietly, and there was no questioning the sincerity of the words. Or the sadness.

Darcy wasn't sure what to make of the sadness...but she was a Collins, and she had not yet begun to fight.

Turning, she smiled at Ryder, letting her expression set his mind at ease. For now. "Don't be sorry, Ryder. You have no reason to be."

He looked like he wanted to argue that fact, but instead he held his piece, then pointed toward the front door. "Looks like our ride is here."

The two of them walked to the car, climbing in the back, explaining to the driver they had two stops.

She was surprised when Ryder reached across the back-seat, taking her hand for a moment and giving it a squeeze.

Darcy squeezed back, depressed when he pulled his grip away again.

Neither of them spoke on the ride to the pub. It was dark inside the bar, though the apartment above was well-lit. Knowing her sister Sunnie, chances were good—blackout or not—the Halloween party had still continued, even though the pub had been forced to close.

"Guess I can't convince you to come up and join the party," she said, not bothering to phrase the words as a request. She knew how he'd respond.

"I think it's better if I head home."

She nodded, getting out of the car. Ryder stepped out as well, looking at the driver. "I'm just going to walk her to the door."

The guy waved, picking up his phone to kill time as he waited.

They walked to the front door of the pub as she searched

for her keys in her purse. Once she had them, she looked at him.

"Tonight was..." He paused and she held her breath, wondering what word he'd use to describe it.

"Don't say fine," she teased.

She smiled when instead, he said, "Surprising. In a good way. A very good way. I'm sorry you were trapped, but I'm glad you were there with me."

"I don't regret anything that happened. I hope you don't, either."

His rueful expression told her he wasn't there yet.

They were silent for a moment, both of them clearly searching for something to say.

"Friends?" he asked tentatively.

They'd never been friends. Not really. But she got a sense he was asking sincerely. "Of course," she said easily, certain that, despite her desire for more, they'd definitely stepped out of that in-between limbo land and crossed the line into a genuine friendship.

He bent down and gave her a quick kiss on the cheek. It wasn't nearly enough and only reminded her exactly what kind of kisses the man was capable of.

"Wait," she whispered when he started to draw away.

Ryder stopped, close enough that she could still feel the heat of his breath on her face, smell the vodka he'd drunk.

"One more real kiss? Please?" She tilted her face up to his, thrilled when he lowered his head and closed the distance. This kiss wasn't as rough or hungry as the ones they'd shared in the elevator. It was softer, sweeter, a little bit sadder, but it still packed a punch.

Ryder pulled away first, pressing his forehead to hers in a gesture that was surprisingly charming. Until he spoke.

"That won't happen again."

His words were firm and spoken with enough conviction that she knew he meant it.

Poor guy.

"Good night, Darcy."

"Good night."

"I'll see you at work on Monday."

She nodded, and once again, Ryder had taken an innocuous statement and provoked two opposing feelings. Monday felt like years away and yet, at the same time, it would be here too damn soon. She needed time to figure out her next move.

He waited until she'd walked inside and locked the door, then she stood in the shadows of the darkened pub and watched as he climbed back in the car.

She sighed heavily as she headed upstairs to the Collins Dorm, the name her mother had given the upstairs apartment she shared with Colm, Gavin, and Oliver.

Sunnie was the only person in the living room, gathering up cups and trash.

"Party over?"

"Yeah. Everyone went home or passed out. Can't guarantee your bed is empty. We all got pretty shit-faced. Hey, where the hell have you been?" her sister asked.

"Power outage. I got stuck in the elevator at work."

Sunnie stopped in mid-clean-up. "Oh my God. Are you okay?"

Darcy nodded. "Yeah. I'm good."

She'd stepped off that elevator determined to go after

what she wanted. Ryder was clearly still devastated by Denise—not just her death but her betrayal as well. And while it had been four years, it didn't look like he had made any strides toward moving on. Instead, he'd buried his head in the sand—or in his case, in work and his sons.

Ryder wasn't going to make it back alone. He needed a shove. And she was just the woman to do it.

"Ryder was with me."

Sunnie's eyes lit up. Her sister suspected her feelings for Ryder, even though Darcy had never come right out and confessed. "Do tell."

Darcy dropped down on the couch. "Oh, Sunnie. He kissed me."

"Whoa." Sunnie put down the empty beer cans she was carrying and joined her on the couch. "And?"

"It was..." Darcy twisted on the couch to face her sister, and she was reminded of the million times previous to this when she and Sunnie would be the only two awake at home. Darcy, three years younger, had always idolized her fun-loving, crazy sister growing up, so she would wait up for Sunnie to get home from her dates, and the two of them would spend the next hour or two dissecting everything that had happened.

"It was..." Sunnie prodded.

"It was fucking amazing."

"It had to be. Ryder's all brooding and mysterious. You just know that guy is alpha from the word go. Believe me, if he hasn't tied a woman up and spanked her ass, he's thought about it a time or twenty. So, what happened after? What did he say?"

"He told me to take off my shirt and bra."

"Shut. Up. He did not!"

Darcy laughed. "Sunnie, I swear to God, I've never been so turned on in my life."

"Did you take them off?"

Darcy tilted her head and narrowed her eyes. "Are you serious? Of course I did. I wasn't born yesterday."

"Then what did he do?"

"I swear it was just like one of those super-sexy movies where the guy can't keep his hands off the girl. He pushed me down to my back and he came over me, kissing me the whole time and—"

"Darcy! Are you still a virgin?"

Darcy grimaced, sighing heavily. "Dammit. Yes. He figured out I didn't have much—any—experience, and he stopped. Said he wasn't going to take me on the floor of an elevator."

"That's sweet. Chivalrous, even."

"Yeah. Lucky me," she replied sarcastically.

"So that was it? Just some hot-and-heavy topless petting?"

Darcy lifted one shoulder, but the casual gesture only piqued her sister's curiosity.

"At what point did he stop?"

Darcy blushed, her grin huge when she said, "He went down on me, and I came so hard, I thought I was going to shatter into a million pieces."

Sunnie—who was never without words—was rendered speechless for a moment, her mouth agape. When she did recover, her response was more breath than sound. "Holy. Fuck."

"I know. But then, like I said, he stopped. Even though I

told him I wasn't saving my virginity for marriage or even love. I just haven't found the right guy."

Sunnie rolled her eyes.

"What?" Darcy asked.

"You've been saving yourself for *him*, Darc. You've been crushing on the guy for years."

"That's not true. It's just..." Darcy didn't have a response for that because her sister had hit the nail on the head.

"None of those idiot drunk frat boys at college ever stood a chance once you laid eyes on Ryder Hagen. You've always been more mature than most kids your age. I assume it's because you were always playing with me and Finn and the older cousins. It's like you skipped ahead a few years or something."

Darcy had never considered it that way, but now that Sunnie pointed it out, that did make sense. Darcy's friend circle was typically always two or more years older than her because the kids in her own grade annoyed the hell out of her.

"The whole night was just so surreal. We played a get-to-know-you game for hours. Asking each other about everything under the sun. He's so incredible, Sunnie. He's smart and passionate about his job and the boys and *Blade Runner*."

Sunnie crinkled her nose in disgust. "That movie sucks. Both versions."

"I know," Darcy said laughing. "I said the same thing. And he's got a sense of humor. A really good one. He's sarcastic, which I love, and he's got this great laugh."

"Wow. Your crush just went full-blown. I think you've crossed into serious infatuation laced with unrequited lust."

Darcy sighed and rested the side of her head on the back of the couch. "Yeah."

"So he didn't just say no to sex on the elevator floor, did he?"

"How did you know?"

Sunnie gave her a slight smile, full of understanding and empathy. "Because there's no way you would look like this after an amazing kiss—and orgasm—with the guy you've been crushing on—"

"Please stop calling it a crush," Darcy urged. "It makes me feel like I'm twelve years old."

"Okay," Sunnie said, revising her previous statement. "You wouldn't look like this after a kiss with the guy you have the hots for if everything ended hunky-dory. Hell, if it had ended perfectly, he would have come up here with you, taken you back to your bedroom, and relieved you of that pesky virginity you don't want."

"That would have been perfect. He said we couldn't do any of that because he's my boss."

"That sounds like an excuse."

"I said that too."

"Isn't that IT girl from work you invited to happy hour here a few weeks ago married to another of the VP's?"

Darcy nodded. "Yeah, she is, but Ryder's still determined that nothing else can happen. Said all we can be is friends."

"Can I ask you something, Darc?"

"Of course."

"Did you see fireworks?"

Sunnie had teased Darcy about her uber-romantic side for years.

"So many fireworks."

"Then don't settle for friendship. I tried to lock Landon in that 'just friends' box. Thank God, he didn't let me get away with it. Think how miserable I'd be right now."

Sunnie had fallen head over heels in love with her best friend, and while the two were happily married now, her sister had definitely given Landon a run for his money.

"All I'm hearing is *my husband is the greatest man on earth*."

Darcy and Sunnie laughed as Landon reached the top of the stairs. He looked beyond exhausted.

"Rough night?" Darcy asked.

"It was a blackout in Baltimore on Halloween, Darc, and I'm a cop. What do you think?"

Sunnie stood up and walked over to him. "Poor baby." She kissed him on the cheek. "I guess I better get this guy home and tuck him into bed with me."

Landon's tiredness seemed to fade a bit as he wiggled his eyebrows suggestively. "All I heard was *bed with you*."

Sunnie grabbed her purse and jacket, turning at the top of the steps to look at Darcy. "Don't give up on him, Darcy."

Darcy smiled, grateful for her sister's encouragement. "I won't. Good night."

Darcy walked to the window, looking out at the dark night, recalling everything she and Ryder had said and done on the elevator. Something told her she'd be reliving tonight over and over and over.

He'd opened up to her, told her things he'd never told another living soul. They'd connected in a very deep and meaningful way.

And then Ryder had closed the door again, tried to chalk

it up to the vodka. He was going to dig his heels in every bit as hard as her sister had with Landon. He was going to come up with a million reasons why the two of them couldn't be together.

Ryder might have finally opened his eyes and seen her as a woman tonight, but he was still blind.

Lucky for him, her vision was twenty-twenty.

CHAPTER FIVE

Ryder pulled into his driveway around nine on Friday night and turned off the car, making no move to get out. Tonight's departure from work was much less eventful than last week's. No power outage, no stuck elevators, no sexy, sweet, innocent Darcy.

He'd been out of the office most of the week, working on-site at the stadium. Today was the only day he'd been in his own office, and even then, he hadn't left it, taking one meeting after another.

One benefit—the primary benefit—of working away from the office was, it made it easy for him to resist the lure of stopping by the marketing department in hopes of seeing Darcy or hearing her infectious laughter.

She'd consumed his thoughts this week, making it hard for him to concentrate on anything else. Something that never happened. His inability to focus was bad enough—his personal assistant, Phillip, had suggested that he get his annual physical, even though it was a few months early. At this rate, he could only assume Phillip was concerned he'd had a series of mini-strokes because it was the only way to explain Ryder acting so completely out of character.

Ryder, who always arrived ten minutes early to everything, had been late to several meetings. He'd also been caught daydreaming on more than one occasion, missing his cue to speak or answer questions directed at him. And Wednesday, he'd worn the exact same suit and tie he'd had on Tuesday.

One night with Darcy was fucking him up.

He'd relived those hours trapped in the elevator more than he cared to admit, and as a result, he'd been dealing with constant, frequent erections. For four years, he'd cursed his impotence.

Now, he'd give anything to return to that state.

He needed to get his head screwed back on straight because even if he was looking for a relationship—which he definitely wasn't—Darcy Young was absolutely, unequivocally wrong for him. She was ten years younger, quick to laugh, a romantic virgin—Jesus, he couldn't begin to wrap his head around that fact—who was looking for true love. To make matters worse, she came from a huge, close-knit family that did everything together.

Ryder hadn't said or done a single romantic thing in his life, his view of the world was cynical and jaded. He was far too rough and demanding in the bedroom to ever introduce an inexperienced woman to sex. And he didn't like people. He barely tolerated them because he was a human on the planet and he *had* to, but just the thought of trying to fit into her loud, boisterous family made his head hurt.

He sighed heavily. It was time for him to put all thoughts

of Darcy out of his head. Time to move on and get back to normal, starting tonight.

He'd go inside, pour himself a bourbon, fire up a movie—not *Blade Runner*, dammit, because it now reminded him of her—and forget last Friday night ever happened.

Satisfied with the plan, he dragged himself from the car and walked into the house. Boomer excitedly greeted him at the door, so he bent down to pat the sweet dog on the head. Loud voices and laughter drifted from the family room.

Great. The boys were knee-deep in one of their damned video games. He longed for a quiet night.

"I'm home," he called out.

He set his briefcase by the door, hung his suit jacket over a chair, and walked into the family room.

And there she was.

It was as if he'd conjured her up merely by thinking about her.

"Darcy?"

She glanced his way briefly before turning her attention back to the TV. "Hey, Ryder. Gimme two seconds. I'm in a bind here."

Ryder took note of her casual, friendly tone. He'd asked for her friendship the night of Halloween. If he'd been smart, he should have suggested things return to normal. Their previous employee/boss relationship would have been easier to maintain. Darcy struck him as the type of woman who took her friendships very seriously.

And while that wasn't a bad thing, he wasn't stupid enough to actually think he'd be able to hang out with her platonically without wanting a hell of a lot of not-just-friends things from her. Not after he'd kissed those soft lips. Or tasted her. Or felt her come apart on his fingers.

Darcy was addictive. And that was a problem.

No amount of labeling the relationship would solve it, either.

She hit the controller like a woman possessed, then groaned, falling back against the couch dramatically. "Dammit. I'm dead."

"Language," Clint said, mimicking the line he'd picked up from Darcy's Pop Pop.

Clint, unlike Vince, was running very low on grandparents, only seeing Denise's parents once or twice a year, whenever they came to Baltimore for a visit. Ryder's parents had seen Clint just one time in his life, when he was still a baby. So, the kid adapted, just like he always did, adopting Darcy's grandfather as her own.

Of course, it was fair to say, Patrick Collins had adopted Clint right back.

Their family dynamics had changed a great deal over the last year or so since Leo and Yvonne had married. Where before, it had been he and Leo raising the boys alone, now, there were three parents in the house. And it worked pretty well.

So well, in fact, he'd named Yvonne and Leo as Clint's guardians in his will because there was no one else he'd want raising his son if anything happened to him.

"Smarty pants," Darcy said, ruffling Clint's hair.

Clint and Vince laughed but kept playing.

"I think these ravenous beasts might have left a few cookies for you. They're in the kitchen."

"Darcy made us chocolate chip cookies," Clint said, his eyes still glued to the game.

"And by made," Darcy said, acting out her words as she explained, "I opened a roll of dough, sliced it, and baked them. I do not have Yvonne's mad skills in the kitchen."

Clint leaned toward her, bumping his shoulder to hers in a friendly, affectionate way. "They were really good."

"They were okay," Vince added, though Ryder could tell from his tone he was teasing Darcy. "Not as good as Vonnie's, but..."

"Kick his butt, Clint," Darcy said as she gestured toward the game.

"Hey," Vince protested. "I was just kidding."

"Doesn't matter, you ruthless fiend. I still haven't forgotten the last game."

Vince grinned, and it was obvious his stepson had beaten her a couple times tonight.

Darcy stood up and walked over to him.

"Leo and Yvonne went out to dinner and a movie. Leo decided to start date night back up. Yvonne's had a hard time separating from Reba, and she's supposed to go back to work next week. He told her tonight would be good practice. Apparently, the Halloween party was a little rocky for her. They got there late because Yvonne was giving her mom seventy-two thousand instructions, then the second the power went out, she helped her dad close the restaurant and bailed on returning to the party in favor of coming back here to Reba. Leo said they weren't away from the baby more than a couple hours. Aunt Natalie was apparently pissed she didn't get more alone time with her granddaughter."

Ryder shook his head, amazed by Darcy's family

dynamics. He and his parents hadn't spoken in years, that silence a blessing. Darcy, on the other hand, always seemed to know everything that was going on in the lives of her relatives.

"Why are you shaking your head?" she asked curiously.

"It's just you and your family...knowing everything about everyone...doesn't that wear you out?"

She looked at him like he was six eggs short of a dozen. "Seriously? Of course not. Would it wear *you* out?"

"I'm not a 'people' person, and every single member of your family is the equivalent of six people in one."

"What do you mean you're not a people person?"

He shrugged. "I don't really like people."

Her eyes widened. "That's the most absurd thing I've ever heard."

"Nevertheless, it's true." Then he added, "Yvonne and Leo should have called me. I would have come—"

Before Ryder could finish speaking, the baby started crying.

"Reba again," Vince said, not bothering to look away from the game, in true teenage, somebody-else's-problem fashion.

"Poor thing is having a hard time settling down tonight." Darcy started down the hall toward the nursery. Ryder stood frozen in the doorway, glancing back at the boys, then in the direction Darcy had gone.

He sighed. "Why don't you guys move the gaming into your bedroom? I'd like to watch some TV before bed."

"Two minutes," Clint said, clearly unwilling to end the game they were currently playing. Ryder also knew two minutes in video-game speak was always closer to fifteen.

"Two minutes," he stressed in his stern dad voice, even though he knew it would do no good.

Ryder drifted down the hall, intent on heading to his room to change into a T-shirt and lounge pants, anxious to shed the suit.

Instead, he followed the sound of Darcy's voice to the nursery.

She was speaking baby talk to the tiny girl, and Ryder couldn't help but grin as he watched her from the doorway to the room.

"Oh my, what a little stinky butt you are. No wonder you couldn't sleep." Darcy reached for a clean diaper. "How in the hell can such a cute baby make such a godawful smell?"

"Should you cuss at a baby?" he murmured from the door.

Darcy glanced over at him and laughed. "I figure I'm safe for a few more months. Do you mind handing me the baby wipes?"

Ryder looked around, spotting the container. He picked it up and walked over to the crib, just halfway there when he stopped in his tracks. His eyes watered at the horrific smell. "Holy mother of God."

Darcy laughed. "Right? And she doesn't even eat real food yet."

Ryder handed her the wipes, then retreated back to the door. "I think I must have blocked out the smells babies make. I swear I don't remember Clint ever stinking up a room like that."

Darcy wiped Reba's tiny bottom and put a clean diaper on, quickly, efficiently, gently. The baby had quit crying as soon as Darcy had the shitty diaper off.

"I'm sure he stunk just as bad. Diapers are probably like childbirth. Parents tend to forget the pain because they're too in love." Darcy picked up Reba, cradling her in her arms, reverting back to baby speak. "I've already forgotten the smelly bottom because who couldn't love this beautiful, sweet, perfect girl?" Darcy continued to coo, swaying back and forth, as Ryder watched. She sat in the rocking chair, slowly lulling the baby back to sleep with gentle motion and soft humming.

It sparked a memory of him doing the same things with Clint when he was a baby—the cooing, the rocking, the singing. He remembered being overwhelmed by so many powerful emotions as he held his son.

Denise had been pregnant when they'd married. Actually, that was why they'd gotten married. They'd been dating for a few months. One night, things had gotten hot and heavy, but he hadn't had a condom. She'd told him she was on birth control and they'd had sex without one.

Denise was the first woman Ryder had ever really dated seriously, the woman and her tiny son, Vince, claiming his playboy heart quickly. So when she'd told him she was pregnant, he'd proposed on the spot.

According to Denise, she'd forgotten to take her pills a couple nights, but she didn't think it would matter. They hadn't dated long enough that he'd been considering marriage, but when she'd told him she was pregnant with his child, something clicked inside him, and Ryder, the man who'd never considered settling down, realized he desperately wanted to be a father.

The months prior to Clint's birth had been tense, to say the least, as they planned a rushed wedding, moved in together, and set up a nursery. Ryder worked from dawn to midnight—both at work, then at their tiny apartment, trying to make sure Denise and Vince had everything they needed. He'd only been twenty-four, the same age Darcy was now, and it felt as if he'd grown up in the blink of an eye, switching from carefree bachelor to family man overnight. Even now, those first months of his marriage were a blur. The only thing Ryder could recall was the exhaustion and the fear of failing Denise and Vince and the baby on the way.

Everything changed when Clint was born and Ryder held his son in his arms for the first time. Those days he remembered as if they'd been imprinted on his brain.

The best way to describe his feelings toward Denise until the doctor placed his son in his hands was genuine affection. However, after he'd looked at Denise, lying in the hospital bed, holding their baby, that changed.

And for the first time in his life, he was in love.

After all, she'd given him the most amazing, incredible gift of his life.

Clint.

All the anxiety and weariness he'd been suffering from faded away that day, replaced by sheer joy.

For a few years, they'd found happiness and managed to forge a family—him, her, Vince, and Clint. He'd landed a great job. They'd bought this house—Denise's dream house— and life had been smooth sailing.

For a while.

Then Denise became distant, distracted, and he, unable to reach her, started to work even longer hours, determined to land the promotion to vice president before he was thirty

—stupidly convinced that more financial security and maybe even a bigger house would help repair their faltering marriage.

Things continued to slip away, the snowball slowly becoming an avalanche.

"I guess it's been an adjustment," Darcy whispered, careful not to disturb Reba. "Having a baby in the house again."

Ryder walked over to where she sat, glancing down at Reba's face. "Not a bad adjustment."

Darcy grinned up at him. "You like babies?"

He nodded, wondering if he'd somehow given Yvonne and Leo the impression that he didn't. Or if there was some other reason they didn't want to leave the baby alone with him. "I love them. Yvonne and Leo could have asked me to come home early tonight. I would have watched her for them so they could go out."

"Are you trying to steal my job?" she teased.

"I'm just saying...I live here and I'm not sure why they..."

Darcy rose slowly, handing him the sleeping baby.

Yvonne was a first-time mother, Leo a hovering and smitten father, Vince and Clint the loving big brothers, so Ryder's opportunities to hold Reba had been few and far between. Somebody else in the family always got there first.

Reba shuffled slightly at the handoff, then settled right back down to sleep. She really was precious. He huffed out a quiet laugh as he looked at the tiny girl.

"Something funny?" Darcy asked curiously.

"You're sharing. Everybody else in this house hogs the baby. I never get a turn."

Darcy's smile grew and he suspected if she weren't

trying to be quiet, she would have barked out one of those loud, infectious laughs of hers. He'd heard it around the office quite a few times over the past couple of months and it never failed to make him grin.

Darcy was very much like his son, Clint. A bundle of positive energy. If they were walking, they were dancing. If they were talking, they were singing.

"Sometimes..." he began, then closed his mouth.

"Yes?" she prodded.

Somewhere along the line, he'd lost the ability to shield his thoughts around Darcy, saying things aloud he never felt compelled to share before. "Sometimes, I feel a bit like the third wheel in this family. Or I should say the sixth wheel?"

"Do you think that's because you spend a lot of time at work? Maybe if you were here more..."

"Yeah. I probably shouldn't complain about not being included in stuff because I'm aware it's my fault."

"That's not what I meant."

"I know that. But the fact is, it's true." Ryder recalled coming home a couple of weeks ago to discover Yvonne had made Clint's Halloween costume for him, and he'd felt guilty because he hadn't even realized the holiday was coming up.

"You should tell Yvonne you wouldn't mind staying alone with Reba. I know she wouldn't have a problem with that at all. I think tonight was more along the lines of she didn't want to impose if you were busy with work. And I also begged to do it."

Ryder nodded, appreciating Darcy's comments. "Okay. I'll tell her."

He shifted toward the crib, carefully putting Reba down. The baby never stirred.

They left the room, walking back toward the family room. Ryder was surprised to discover Vince and Clint clearing out as he'd asked.

"Where are you guys going?" Darcy asked.

"Video games in our room," Vince answered. "Ryder wants the TV."

"Gotcha. I'll come in before I leave to say goodbye," she said.

Ryder considered telling her she didn't need to stay, but he didn't want her to leave yet.

Vince and Clint continued to their room.

"Want a glass of wine?" Ryder asked.

Darcy's expression brightened as if he'd offered her a diamond necklace. "That would be great. Thanks."

She followed him to the kitchen, grabbing two wineglasses from the cabinet while he opened a bottle of Chardonnay, then poured. Darcy was completely at home in his house, something he knew but had never really paid attention to.

They returned to the family room. Darcy claimed her previous spot on one end of the couch, so Ryder took the other side. If he were less of a sadomasochist, he would have chosen the recliner, which was well away from her, instead of sitting so closely, knowing he couldn't kiss her.

Now he was close enough to catch a whiff of her coconut-scented hair.

Darcy took a sip of the wine before setting it on the end table. She sighed, looking completely relaxed.

Ryder longed for that same feeling, but ever since finding

her in his house, his body had betrayed him, going on full alert. He'd spent the last seven days walking around at half-mast, thanks to Darcy flooding his brain.

Sitting next to her now had his cock rock hard and aching.

They sat in silence for a couple minutes, but it didn't feel awkward.

Finally, Darcy turned to him. "Looks like we've hit that point in our relationship where we've run out of things to talk about."

Ryder nodded. "It was inevitable."

Darcy's eyes were pure mischief when she said, "But at least we'll always have those three magical hours in the elevator. We had a good run, you and me."

"That we did." Ryder enjoyed their banter. There weren't too many people in his life he joked around with. As the boss, employees tended to be on their most professional behavior around him. And unfortunately, the rest of the people in upper management were stuffy assholes.

Ryder considered that...and realized he probably fell into that category as well.

So, with the exception of Darcy and the boys, there wasn't a lot of playfulness in Ryder's life.

"You were absent from the office a lot this week," Darcy mused.

He was secretly—foolishly—pleased she'd missed him. "I was working at the stadium."

"Yeah. That's what Helen said. I was sort of hoping you were playing hooky for a few days."

"I don't play hooky."

"You know," she began, "there's a saying about all work and no play."

"I believe I've heard that expression before."

She sat with one leg tucked under the other, her tight jeans fitting her like a second skin. He imagined himself reaching over to peel them off her so he could run his hands over her firm calf muscles and push her thighs—

Mercifully, Darcy interrupted that fantasy before it went way too far. "Don't you ever get sick of wearing ties?"

Ryder had intended to change into more comfortable clothing, but he'd been distracted by her and the baby. He loosened his tie, swallowing deeply when Darcy shifted closer, untying the knot completely and pulling it off him. Once again, her actions felt vaguely familiar. Especially when he took the tie from her, slowly wrapping it around his palm, recalling her desire to be tied up in bed.

Darcy watched his actions, and he could tell her thoughts were traveling along the same path. Especially when her tongue darted out to wet her lower lip.

He'd told her they wouldn't kiss again, and he'd meant it. At the time.

Now, a week had passed and proven his willpower wasn't as strong as he'd thought.

He took a deep breath, then tossed the tie onto the coffee table.

Darcy leaned forward and unbuttoned the top button of his shirt, as if it was completely normal for her to do so, and again, he had this sense that they'd been here, done this before.

The words "don't stop" flashed through his mind and sparked a memory.

"You've done that before," he whispered.

"I didn't think you remembered that night. You were very drunk."

That night.

Suddenly, things clicked into place. Ryder didn't recall much at all, nothing more than images and the impression of not being alone for the first time in a long time. The first year or so after Denise died had been one long, dark period of time where the only thing he'd felt was unbearable loneliness. Darcy had taken care of him that night.

"Darcy..." he started. But she didn't give him a chance to finish. Which was good because he wasn't sure what he wanted to say anyway.

"I've been thinking," she said, lowering her hands after unbuttoning just that one button on his shirt.

He groaned. "Why do I get the sense this isn't going to bode well for me?"

"Clint's eleven now."

"I know. I was there when he was born."

Darcy ignored his joke. "You're getting perilously close to that time when he'll suddenly be too cool to want to do stuff with his dad."

Ryder nodded slowly. He'd begun to witness that with Vince and Leo. Vince hit puberty and became a moody bastard. The boy's eye-rolling and persecuted sighs drove Leo insane.

Clint, however, still approached most days with a child-like wonder and excitement. Just last weekend, Ryder had suggested they throw the football around in the backyard because he wanted to unplug the kid from the video games for a few minutes. He'd also figured the activity would help divert his own thoughts from Darcy.

Clint had perked up instantly, shut down mid-game—something unheard of—and they'd spent nearly two hours outside, playing, roughhousing, laughing. It had been one of the best afternoons the two of them had spent in ages.

"What are you saying, Darcy?"

"Hand off some of the easier stuff at work. Let someone else do it so you're home earlier and more often. I'm afraid you'll look back thirty years from now and regret working so much."

Ryder considered her advice. The crazy thing was, he'd never been accused of working too hard before he and Denise married. He'd been an immature, party-'til-you-drop frat guy, who luckily was intelligent enough that hours and hours of studying weren't vital to his GPA.

He'd met Denise in a local bar shortly after completing his MBA. She hadn't attended college, but instead still lived with her parents and worked part-time at a local restaurant, waiting tables while raising her young son.

After they married, Ryder worked fairly long hours because he didn't want to fail his family. Denise had wanted to quit her waitressing job to be a stay-at-home mom, something they both agreed was best for the kids. But that had meant it was up to him to keep them afloat financially. Even so, he'd still managed to be home for dinner most every night. Something he'd done less and less in the past few years.

"I've gotten into some bad habits," he admitted. "I mean, I've always worked a lot, but I started working longer hours just before Denise died and then after, it got worse because..." Ryder rubbed his eyes wearily, debating whether or not he wanted to finish that statement.

Of course, Darcy didn't give him a bye.

"Because?" Darcy asked quietly.

"Because I'd gone to a dark place. A really dark place, and I didn't want Clint and Vince to see that."

"Dark?" she whispered.

"I was depressed and angry and I couldn't find my way back. I was terrified my feelings would rub off on the boys. That they'd sense my bitterness and rage and, I don't know, feed on it. They both loved their mother, and I was struggling to shield..." He sighed and let it drop there.

"I get it." Darcy could speak volumes with just her eyes. They expressed so many things, she never needed to speak. Right now, she looked sad, and he hated that he'd started this whole conversation.

She'd unlocked something in that elevator, and now he was spilling his guts to her at every turn like she was a priest in a confessional, or a shrink.

He wasn't a talker—not socially, and sure as fuck not about his emotions. His mother had called him a stoic once, but she hadn't meant it as a compliment. She'd used the word when comparing him to his emotionally distant, cold father. It was meant to sting. And it did.

"Leo was here and he was...he was in a better headspace, a better father."

Darcy shook her head. "No. You're both great fathers. Never say anything different. I won't hear it."

His lips quirked. There'd been precious little to smile about for so long that sometimes Ryder thought he'd forgotten how. But Darcy always managed to draw two or twenty smiles out of him whenever they were talking.

"Are you still in that dark place?" she asked.

He stroked his beard, wishing he'd kept his damn mouth shut. He hated talking about shit like this.

"Ryder?" she pressed, forcing himself to consider her question.

Was he in a dark place? It occurred to him if she'd asked him a year ago, he would have said yes without hesitation. But lately, he noticed the weight that had been crushing him since Denise's death wasn't there anymore. He wouldn't call himself the happiest guy on the planet, but he wasn't angry, or even hurt. It seemed somewhere along the line, he'd simply let all of that go.

Then he recalled the get-to-know-you game they'd played in the elevator. And tossing the football around with his son. And holding Reba just a few minutes earlier.

The last week had actually been...fun.

He shook his head. "No. I'm not."

Darcy smiled. "Good. I'm glad. So you don't have to avoid this house and the people in it by working all the time. It's time to have a life. Start dating. I know this adorable brunette in the marketing department at work. I could totally set you up."

He shook his head, even though her offer had definitely woken his libido. "Nice try, Buttercup."

Darcy giggled. "I'm sure you didn't mean that as a term of endearment, but I'm taking it as one anyway. Think about it. We could help each other out in terms of our somewhat similar problems."

"Similar problems?"

"I have this virginity I'm dying to get rid of, and I think you're definitely in the mood to end your long dry spell."

Ryder groaned. "Jesus. Please don't paint those pictures in my head."

She laughed. "But they're so pretty."

"Did I say tenacious before?"

"You did."

"Yeah. I think it bears repeating."

Darcy reached over and lightly smacked him on the arm, and he shook his head at her playful touch.

Unable to resist, Ryder reached out and tugged her hair, the action meant to mimic hers—all in fun. Until he touched her long, silky strands...and held on.

Darcy's eyes closed briefly, and he recalled her desires.

He tugged it harder and caught her soft intake of breath. *Shit. Abort. Abort.*

He forced himself to release his grip. "You have very soft hair."

Darcy shifted closer, running her fingers over the side of his face, touching his close-cropped beard. "Yours is coarse. It tickled when..."

Her flush told him exactly when and where his beard had tickled her. He gripped her wrist.

"Still playing the boss card?" she asked.

"I still *am* the boss."

A voice in his head was telling him to let go, but instead, he interlocked his fingers with hers. And he didn't move away when Darcy shifted even closer.

Too close.

Not close enough.

"Darcy," he murmured, intent on repeating the same

damn thing he had last week. The words fell away when she cupped his face with her free hand, her thumb lightly stroking his beard once more.

It had been too long since he'd felt desire. Fuck, since he'd felt anything that wasn't either rage, despair, or numbness.

Darcy made him feel too many things...all at once. It was a jumble inside. And right now, the only thing he could focus on was how much he wanted to kiss her again.

So he made yet another mistake, as he leaned forward to capture her lips.

Darcy met him halfway and after that, he was lost to anything and everything that wasn't her.

He grasped her waist, tugging her toward him. Darcy followed the direction of his grip, shifting until she straddled him, their lips never parting.

Their mouths opened, and he found her tongue, her teeth, stealing a taste of the wine she'd been drinking and the heat of her sweet breath.

Her hand drifted around his neck as her hips gyrated, pressing her pussy against his crotch.

What would he give to divest them both of their pants and push inside her tight—fuck, *virgin*—

Ryder broke the kiss, lifting Darcy off his lap just as headlights flashed through the window.

Darcy sat next to him, looking somewhat dazed—and disappointed.

"Looks like Leo and Yvonne are home." It was clear from her tone she knew that wasn't the reason why he'd broken off their kiss.

"I'm sorry, Darcy. I realize I'm giving you mixed signals.

Saying something, then doing something completely different."

She gave him one of her endearing grins. "So start saying the things that match those amazing kisses and we'll be fine."

He heard the car doors slam. He only had a few seconds to try to make this right. It was on the tip of his tongue to tell her that was the last time, that it wouldn't happen again, but he'd already told that lie once, and even now, his resistance was weak.

All he could think about was dragging Darcy to his bedroom and tying her to his bed until he fucked out this uncontrollable hunger for her. Shouldn't take more than a year or eighteen, he figured.

"I can't do that. I know what you want, and I can assure you, I'm not that man. I'm sorry, but I'm just not," he admitted, because what he wanted and what Darcy wanted were worlds apart. He wanted her physically, so badly it hurt. However, Darcy was looking at him with those soulful blue eyes, seeing someone who didn't exist.

She wanted a prince.

He was a frog.

CHAPTER SIX

—————————

"**W**ell now, that's a long face, lass. Where's that bright smile of yours?"

Darcy offered her grandfather a half-hearted attempt as she climbed onto the stool next to his regular spot at the pub. It was a Sunday afternoon, and the regular crowd gathered to watch, discuss, and place wagers on the football games. She'd been watching the Ravens play upstairs with Colm, Kelli, Oliver, and Gavin, but she couldn't get into the game, so she'd decided to seek out Pop Pop. He always knew how to cheer her up when she was low.

Her cousin Padraig was tending bar. He came over with a pint of Guinness for Pop Pop. "Want something, Darc?"

"A glass of Chardonnay. Or maybe a bottle."

Padraig chuckled. "You gotta stop hanging out with Kelli so much. She's a bad influence on you."

Once Padraig had delivered her glass—he refused to leave the bottle—he continued along the bar, refilling and taking orders. The pub always did a great business on football days.

"So, are you going to tell me what's got you down?"

"Are you sure you don't mind talking? I know the game is on."

Pop Pop gave her a look that told her she should know better. "I've seen thousands of football games, Darcy. It won't hurt me to miss a wee bit of this one. Besides, the Ravens are winning."

She grinned. Her grandfather was a hardcore Baltimore fan—across the board. If Baltimore had a team, Pop Pop bled for them.

"There's this guy I'm interested in," she started.

Pop Pop instantly smiled. She got her hopeless romantic genes from him. There was nothing the man loved more than a love story.

Not that she was anywhere near that yet with Ryder. He'd spent the entire week working at the stadium *again*, and she suspected it was because he was trying to avoid her. Especially when Helen mentioned in passing how strange it was for him to be out of the office so much.

"Tell me all about him."

"Actually, I've known him for years. So have you."

Pop Pop studied her face intently, nodding. "I see. You're finally ready to admit that you're smitten with Ryder."

Darcy sighed heavily, considering Ryder's observation about her family knowing everyone else's business. She was starting to think maybe that wasn't always a good thing. "Does everyone in the family know?"

Pop Pop chuckled. "Only the ones who've been paying attention. So yes, I venture to guess everyone knows."

"At least smitten is a better word than crush."

"But the real question is *how* smitten. Twittery stomach?"

She laughed. "Check."

"Sweaty palms?"

"Again, check."

"How about that heart?"

"Races a million miles a minute whenever he's around."

Pop Pop's grin faded. "So am I to assume from your sad expression and heavy sighs that your feelings aren't returned?"

Darcy shrugged. Because the truth of the matter was there were times—brief moments—when she thought Ryder did have feelings for her. Then he'd shutter them away behind that stupid "I'm the boss" excuse.

Which he and Darcy both knew wasn't the real reason he was pushing her away. Ryder's reluctance to pursue a relationship was based on past history, and Darcy wasn't sure that was something she could defeat. Especially not with Ryder digging his heels in and avoiding her like the plague.

"Why didn't you ever remarry after Grandma Sunday passed away?"

If Pop Pop was surprised by her abrupt left turn, he didn't show it. "That's an interesting question. One I've had quite a few decades to consider. And the answer might surprise you."

Darcy twisted on her stool to face him. "Surprise me?"

"The easy answer is, she was my true love, the one my heart beat for, and no one else could ever take her place."

Darcy tried to understand why he thought that would

shock her. "Are you saying that isn't the answer? Because that's what I would have expected you to say."

"She was all that to me, Darcy. She absolutely was. But..." Pop Pop glanced over his shoulder. Padraig was leaning against the counter at the end of the bar, talking to Emmy, a romance writer and regular at the pub.

"But..." Darcy prodded.

"In the past, I've always said she was my *one* true love. The only one for me. I don't say that anymore because..."

"Because Paddy's always listening." Her cousin, Padraig, had married his true love, Mia. And for one year, they'd lived a lifetime of love before she'd passed away—too young—from a brain tumor.

Pop Pop turned and smiled at her. "He is. When you get to be my age, you have a lot of time to look back over your life, to consider decisions you made, paths you walked. You can acknowledge regrets and either do something about them or let them go. And if there's one thing I've discovered, there's *never* one thing driving a person's decisions, but a million little things. I didn't remarry after Sunday because my heart was shattered, but also because I had seven children and a business to run. Dating wasn't something I had time for, even if I wanted to, so I shut that part down."

"Do you regret that?"

"I don't. But I will regret it if Padraig follows in my footsteps. I no longer believe there is just one true love for each of us, but instead, a multitude of possibilities for genuine happiness and love. My heart didn't truly stop beating when Sunday died, but I believed it did. I wonder sometimes if there had been an Emmy sitting at the end of the bar over the years, and I failed to see her because I'd blinded myself to not only love but to hope."

Darcy leaned back, moved by her grandfather's words. "So you believe it's possible for someone to love more than once?"

"I was much older when I lost Sunday. We'd shared thirty years together. That was not enough years for me, but it was a lifetime compared to what Ryder shared with his bride. What Paddy had with Mia. They are both young men, and there are far too many things they are going to miss out on if they...well, if they can't give their hearts to another. Ryder has your heart, doesn't he?"

Darcy nodded. "You said you knew you loved Grandma the night you met her."

"I did. I did indeed."

"I'm younger than Ryder. Ten years younger. And everyone keeps calling this a crush, which makes it sound like something silly that I'll get over eventually."

"I don't believe it's a crush."

This was why Darcy had sought out her grandfather. He never belittled her feelings. He always took what she said seriously.

"I was only twenty when I met Sunday, and she was but nineteen. Age means nothing when it comes to matters of the heart."

"Was there anything someone could have done to open your eyes after Grandma Sunday passed away?" she asked.

"Ryder is still grieving for his wife?"

Darcy didn't know how to answer that because she wasn't sure how Ryder felt about Denise. His story had ended much differently than Pop Pop's, but Darcy wouldn't share that with her grandfather. It wasn't her secret to share, and she would never betray Ryder's trust.

Prior to their conversation in the elevator, she had assumed Ryder was in the same boat as Padraig, still grieving. But then he revealed Denise's betrayal, and now Darcy couldn't decide if he was avoiding relationships because of a broken heart or because of wounded pride. Or, most likely, both.

He insisted he didn't believe in love and romance. What she couldn't figure out was if he'd always felt that way or if his feelings had changed after Denise's death.

Because of the way things ended, it was clear Ryder's feelings about his late wife had run the gamut from red-hot rage to gut-wrenching sorrow to zombie-like numbness over the past four years. Darcy suspected there was a broken heart buried beneath that hodge-podge of emotion, but Ryder's pride wouldn't accept that, wouldn't face it.

Of course, she also couldn't dismiss the fact he'd proclaimed he was thirty-four and that he'd never seen fireworks or found true love.

The only thing that was clear to her was Ryder seemed to believe his life was fine just the way it was, and she desperately wanted to prove him wrong.

"She's been gone four years." That wasn't an answer, but it was all Darcy had.

"You care deeply for the man."

Darcy nodded, even though Pop Pop hadn't asked a question.

"And Clint."

She smiled. "He's an amazing boy. I love him. And Vince, even though he's become a grumpy bastard."

Pop Pop grinned. "Puberty does a number on otherwise pleasant young boys."

They sat in silence for a few minutes until finally Pop Pop reached over and placed his hand on hers. She glanced down at his gnarled fingers and wrinkled skin, always amazed by the strength and the warmth in his old hands.

"Open his eyes, Darcy. If anyone can warm a lonely heart, it's you, my dear."

Pop Pop always knew exactly what to say, always found a way to bolster her wavering confidence. It was another reason she'd sought him out today. Not seeing Ryder this past week had given her too much time to fret and question everything.

She smiled. "I hope that's true."

"Never doubt it, lovely girl. Never doubt it."

RYDER LOWERED the footrest on the recliner as soon as the football game ended. He had a shit-ton of chores to take care of around the house, but the idea of actually doing them seemed beyond him at the moment.

He sighed heavily.

"You okay?"

He glanced over at Leo, who was sprawled out on the couch, looking just as unenergetic as he felt. Yvonne was working at the pub today, and the boys were somewhere outside, playing with a bunch of the neighborhood kids. Reba was napping in her crib.

It was on the tip of Ryder's tongue to give Leo his standard "I'm fine" response, but he didn't. Ever since he'd kissed

Darcy—again—on the couch Leo was now sitting on, he'd been kicking his own ass, half the time for kissing her, the other half for pushing her away.

He'd taken the coward's way out all week, opting to work at the stadium again—for the second week in a row—something he couldn't continue to do. This coming week he was going to have to bite the bullet and return to the office.

He felt the need to talk about some of the shit rumbling around in his head, and Leo was the closest thing he had to a friend. "I need some advice."

Leo's raised eyebrows spoke to how seldom Ryder asked for personal help. "You got it. What's up?"

"I can't seem to stop kissing Darcy."

"Yvonne's *cousin* Darcy?" Leo's mild astonishment over Ryder asking for advice was nothing compared to his outright shock now.

"We got trapped in the elevator at work on Halloween, during that power outage. One thing led to another, and I kissed her."

"Wow. Have to admit I didn't see that coming. I mean, I've always sort of suspected Darcy had a thing for you, a crush or something, but you've never seemed interested in dating."

Ryder *wasn't* interested in dating, but that wasn't the part of Leo's statement that caught his attention. "A crush?"

Leo shrugged casually. "She's never said anything. Neither has Yvonne. It's just a feeling I got whenever I saw you two together."

"Do you think she's too young for me?"

Leo shook his head. "No. I don't think age matters. You're both adults. Is that what's bothering you?"

"No. It's not." He was latching onto the age thing as an excuse—a lame one at that. The more time he spent with Darcy, the more he found himself struggling to recall that she was younger. And he hadn't thought of her as the babysitter since Halloween.

Leo leaned forward. "So that *can't stop kissing her* comment makes me think these make-out sessions weren't limited to the elevator."

"I'm attracted to her. I haven't felt that spark toward a woman since..."

Leo nodded in understanding. He didn't need to hear the words. "Denise has been gone four years, Ryder. To some, that might seem like a long time, but if you don't think you're ready to move on—"

"That's not—" Ryder stopped himself mid-sentence, very nearly confessing it wasn't Denise's death, but her betrayal that had kept him from seeking out other women. That and the goddamned impotence he hadn't managed to overcome until...Darcy. "That's not a problem."

"Is it Clint holding you back? Because I'll admit, I had those same concerns about Vince when I started dating Yvonne. It's hard to start a relationship when there's a kid involved, you know. I mean, if things go south, it's not just your heart that's broken."

In truth, Ryder hadn't even considered that argument because before he'd started this conversation with Leo, he'd been dead set against dating Darcy, period. But now...it felt like he *was* actually considering it. "I hadn't thought about that. Clint adores Darcy. Maybe I shouldn't disrupt the status quo, because I wouldn't want to jeopardize their relationship. If things didn't work out—"

"I don't think that's something you have to worry about," Leo interjected. "Darcy's crazy about the boys, and I can't see her walking away from them, even if things between you two didn't work out. Plus, with Yvonne and I living here—"

"Darcy would still come over to visit."

"Yeah. She would. She's family. Ryder...what is it that's bothering you about this?"

"I know what Darcy wants from a relationship, and I'm not sure I'm capable of giving it to her."

"What does she want?"

"Love. Romance. Forever."

Leo leaned back, frowning slightly. "Were you and Denise happy together?"

Leo's question blindsided him.

Denise was one topic neither of them had ever broached with each other. Leo had dated Denise all through high school, and her pregnancy with Vince hadn't been planned. Leo had proposed to her on the spot, just as Ryder had when she'd told him she was pregnant with Clint. However, she'd rejected Leo's proposal.

Ryder had had a lot of time to reflect on Denise's character the past few years, looking at her through a veil of anger, and the picture he'd painted of her wasn't a pretty one. After high school graduation, Leo was going to work on the family farm, college not part of his plans. Denise was obviously aiming higher.

He recalled that she'd been very impressed by his MBA, and after they married, her desire for the big house, the brand-new car, the designer clothes, proved that money mattered quite a lot to her. It was the main thing they consistently fought over because her spending was frequently out of hand.

Now, he was beginning to see a lot of that was his fault, as well. He'd been raised by two workaholic parents, who proved their love not through affection or closeness but through financial security. He'd never thought—never wanted—to be like them, but when he looked back now, he wondered if Denise had spent so much money, and then sought out someone else, because he'd been so emotionally distant, his wallet open, but his heart...not so much.

"I thought we were, but..." Ryder shook his head. "Toward the end...no. We weren't happy."

"I always wondered."

"Had a feeling about that too?" Ryder asked.

"What can I say? I'm deep."

The two of them laughed, and Ryder realized this conversation had helped. He wasn't feeling quite as stressed out.

"So...are you going to date Darcy?" Leo asked.

If he was a wise man, he'd walk into work tomorrow and tell Darcy they couldn't be anything more than friends, but Ryder knew he'd never get the words out. The simple truth was, he wanted her. And, for some insane reason, she wanted him.

"I wish I knew," he admitted. "Hey, do me a favor. Don't mention this to Yvonne. Just in case I come to my senses."

Leo pretended to lock his lips and toss away the key. "It's in the vault. But I'll warn you now, secrets don't exist in the Collins family. So if you do decide to date her, don't get too set on keeping the relationship quiet. Oh, and you might want to clear your social calendar. The Collins clan does the holidays right."

"They do like to party, don't they?"

Leo's smile filled his face, making it clear he didn't have a problem with Yvonne's large, loud, rowdy family. "I don't mean to put the cart before the horse, but I hope you decide to go out with her, Ryder. The more I think about it, the more I think Darcy's perfect for you."

Ryder couldn't begin to figure out why Leo would think so, but before he could ask, Clint and Vince returned and the conversation ended.

He forced himself up and managed to accomplish about a quarter of the things on his Sunday to-do list. Throughout the day, he mentally compiled a pros and cons list in regards to Darcy.

The cons list was fairly substantial and included the boss situation, Clint, Darcy's family, her beliefs about true love and romance, the age difference, and the fact he was bound and determined to remain single 'til death did he depart...alone.

The pros list was much less impressive. In fact, there was only one thing encouraging him to pursue her.

Darcy, herself.

Because the simple truth was...he was enthralled by her, attracted to her, drawn to her.

And no matter how many excuses—lame or otherwise—filled the cons side, he knew he wouldn't—couldn't—stay away.

CHAPTER SEVEN

Ryder swiveled away from his desk in his leather office chair so he could face the large windows that overlooked the city. His office door was open and Darcy's voice drifted down the hall. She was talking with two of her colleagues just outside the conference room, following Helen's weekly department meeting.

It was Friday again. And this week had been even more fucked up than the previous two. If things kept up like this, not only would his personal assistant, Phillip, quit, but Ryder would be fired.

The worst day had been yesterday when Helen asked Darcy to assist her in presenting the graphics they'd created for a corporate holiday party, and Ryder had missed a large chunk of what was said.

Instead, he'd been obsessing over Darcy's perfume, wondering what the scent was and where she'd daubed it—her wrists, her neck? Then he'd imagined seeking that answer out, drawing his nose and lips over her bare skin until he found the spot where the smell was strongest and kissing her there.

Since then, he'd decided he was suffering from a midlife crisis, and he had actually spent the better part of his lunch hour today looking at sports cars. He'd be willing to indulge any cliché if it helped him find a way to get the pretty young woman currently laughing down the hall out of his head.

Unfortunately, he'd had to work at the office all week, rather than the stadium, and it seemed like every time he turned around, Darcy was there. Probably because they kept finding ways to seek each other out.

Monday, he'd followed her to the coffee machine and they'd chatted briefly. Tuesday, she'd stopped by his office to invite him to grab a sandwich at the café on the first floor with her and a couple of other people in the office for lunch. He'd surprised himself—and their colleagues—by accepting, and for the first time in forever, he'd taken a lunch break that wasn't connected to a meeting for work. And enjoyed it.

On Wednesday, she'd gone for broke and convinced him to knock off work early—which meant on time—to join her for a quick happy hour at Pat's Pub. The two of them had kicked back at the counter with her grandfather and best friend, Brooklyn, drinking a couple pints of Guinness each and polishing off a large order of cheese fries.

Yesterday, he'd decided the madness had to stop, and he had turned down her invitation to karaoke. Then he'd spent the whole night at home, on the couch, wondering what song she was singing and regretting his decision not to go listen.

So it was time to give in and admit this wasn't going away. No matter how much he tried to pretend it might.

The worst part was, Darcy wasn't only taking over his

days, she'd claimed all his nights and cost him more hours of sleep than he could count. He'd played out so many sexual fantasies about her the last three weeks, his dick was actually sore from all the jerking off. It was as if he was making up for the past four years all in one fell swoop.

No. Not four years.

Five years.

That epiphany had hit him last night as he was taking his second cold shower of the evening.

He and Denise hadn't had sex in the year prior to her death, which made sense, now that he knew she was having an affair. Back then...well, back then, he hadn't given it much thought because he'd been too busy with work.

Spending all this time with Darcy seemed to be awakening memories of Denise, things he'd pushed down deep and refused to look at. Things he wasn't particularly proud of. Things that proved he shouldn't be taking lunch breaks and doing happy hours with the twenty-four-year-old graphic artist down the hall.

He wasn't the type of guy who could do romance or true love, given the fact he hadn't even fallen in love with his wife until he'd seen her holding his son. He'd inherited more of his parents' attributes than he cared to admit. After all, his mother and father put their jobs ahead of everything, including the rearing of their son. Ryder had been dropped off at daycare, starting when he was just four weeks old, and it hadn't been unusual for him to be the first kid there in the morning and the last to leave each evening.

His father had never tossed a football with him and had actually been out of town on a business trip the day Ryder graduated from high school. In his parents' minds, providing for him financially was more than enough to prove they cared about him, and it never occurred to either of them that he might need something like love or affection.

After high school, Ryder had chosen to attend school on the East Coast, desperate to make the break from his parents once and for all. They'd paid his way through school, never once blinking an eye that he chose to spend holidays and summers with friends. He hadn't been back to the house he'd grown up in once since leaving for college. And his parents had only seen Clint after he was born because they'd both had business trips near Maryland and managed to squeeze in a short visit to see their grandchild. That was the first and last time they'd seen Clint.

The only time Ryder had heard from them in the past decade was when they sent a sympathy card after Denise's death.

A fucking sympathy card.

He knew it wasn't uncommon for children to follow in their parents' footsteps, but Ryder had always sworn he'd do better. Be better.

With Denise, he'd failed. Miserably. Expecting his paycheck to be enough to pass as proof of love.

To make matters worse, Darcy's childhood had been the polar opposite of his. She was a Collins, a name synonymous for large, loving, in-each-other's-business-all-the-damn-time family, so God only knew what she'd think of his fucked-up family tree.

The second he thought of her, his dick twitched.

Jesus.

He was more than his penis. He was an adult, and he should be able to control these baser desires.

He closed his eyes, rubbing them wearily. He was about to make a huge mistake—and even though he recognized that, he didn't bother to stop himself from making it.

Spinning his chair back toward his desk, he picked up his phone, dialing her extension.

"Darcy Young," she said, obviously before glancing at the caller ID on her work phone. "Oh, Ryder. Hey. What's up?"

"Can you come to my office for a few minutes?"

"Sure. Do you need me to bring anything?"

He'd never summoned her to his office once in the past three months she'd worked here, so she obviously thought this had something to do with the job.

He wished he could be that fucking professional right now.

"No." He disconnected the call, then watched the door.

The marketing department was fairly close, so she was there within a minute or two.

"Shut the door," he said the second she crossed the threshold. "And lock it."

Darcy froze for a split second, her gaze locking with his. Then, she grinned and did exactly as he asked.

He rose from his chair and crooked his finger at her. "Come here."

He'd resisted kissing her for two whole weeks. He was calling that a victory.

Of course, he was about to have to restart the clock.

Darcy crossed the office, stopping a few feet in front of him.

He shook his head. "Closer."

She glanced over her shoulder at the locked door, then closed the distance between them.

Ryder wasted no time gripping her upper arms and pulling her the rest of the way toward him, lowering his head and kissing her hard. Darcy, as always, was an active, enthusiastic participant. She kissed like she lived—with exuberance and joy.

He felt the ends of her lips tip up in a smile as her tongue darted out to play with his. At one point, she even nipped his bottom lip, giggling when he narrowed his eyes at the brief pain.

She tucked her hands beneath his suit jacket, her fingers gripping his dress shirt at his midsection. Meanwhile, he couldn't manage to touch her enough. He ran his fingers through her hair, then cupped the nape of her neck to deepen the kiss. After that, his hands drifted lower along her back, to her waist, to her hips. She gasped slightly when he dropped them even farther and gripped her ass.

Darcy was the first to pull away slightly, sucking in a deep breath of air. Ryder wasn't ready to stop, so he placed kisses on her cheek, along her neck.

"Is this going to be our thing?" Darcy asked breathlessly. "Friday kisses? Because I'm totally cool with branching out and including a few more days of the week. Maybe Mondays? Wednesdays? Every day that ends in Y? You missed last Friday, by the way, so you owe me extra kisses."

Ryder wasn't ready to talk. Talking required thinking and thinking led to common sense and reality. He wasn't willing to go there yet. He kissed her again, trying to understand what it was about this woman that had him acting like a horny teenager on his first date. He was a grown-ass, reasonable, responsible man, who'd never had trouble remaining in control.

"Darcy," he whispered. "I think you've put a spell on me."

"No. Not a spell. But I'm sort of hoping I've cursed you."

He lifted his head, confused. "A curse? That would be worse than a spell."

She shrugged casually. "Depends on who you ask, I guess."

He squeezed her ass cheeks one last time, then forced himself to take a step away.

"Are we already to the part where you tell me why we shouldn't do this?" she asked. "Because I'm aware you're still the boss." He could tell she was only half-teasing, which reminded him that it wasn't just him he was fucking up with this kiss-and-run game.

"I've been thinking about you the past couple of weeks."

"Ditto."

"I've been thinking about our similar problems," he began.

She laughed. "Okay."

"I think it's obvious that I'm attracted to you. That's not something I've experienced with another woman in a long time. But, Darcy, you've never—"

"Stop. I know what you're going to say, Ryder, and I don't know how to convince you that I haven't been saving myself. Honestly."

"Regardless, a woman's first time should be special, and it should be with someone she cares about."

"I care about *you.*"

He wasn't sure how to respond to that...because it had

become very clear to him since that night in the elevator that he cared about Darcy too. That he had for years. Of course, rather than make this discussion easy, it made it more difficult.

Because they weren't just talking about sex. If they were, this conversation wouldn't even be necessary. They'd fall into bed together until this spell—or curse—was broken, then part as friends at the end. No muss, no fuss.

But that wasn't what she wanted. Darcy wanted to date him, and she definitely fell into that category of women looking for a relationship that would lead to marriage.

That thought alone should have him saying forget it and sending her back to her desk.

Instead, he reached out and ran the backs of his fingers down her cheek gently. She was so fucking beautiful, she took his breath away.

"I care about you too, Buttercup. But...well...there's a lot at stake, and I'm not so sure we'd be smart to cross a line we couldn't cross back over if—"

"So we lower the stakes."

He shook his head. "I don't think that's possible."

"You keep dismissing this out of hand. What about a trial run?" she asked. "We go out a few times and give each other a taste of what it would be like if we were together."

"Isn't that basically what all dating is? A trial run?" he asked.

"All I'm saying is we give this a try. This doesn't have to be life altering or scary. We just...go out, have fun, see if we fit. If we don't, we shift right back to being friends again."

No commitment, just a trial. It would give him a chance to get Darcy out of his system. He knew that wasn't her intention, but to Ryder, it felt like the answer to a prayer because it would accomplish two things.

One, it would return him to solid ground, give him a chance to screw his head back on, because he knew—deep down—he was meant to live an unencumbered life. The problem was it had been too long since he'd been with a woman and it was messing with his head, making him think he wanted something he didn't.

And two, it would show Darcy he wasn't the man she thought he was. Romance wasn't his forte, and that would become obvious pretty quickly. They could chalk it up as a failed experiment and move on without regrets or the shadow of "what if" constantly lurking over their heads.

"Okay. I like that idea."

She grinned. "Ah, but that's only because you haven't heard what my plan for the first date is."

He narrowed his eyes. "Does it require that I rent a limo?"

"Shit, I forgot about that. Not this first one, but I'm not ruling that out for another date."

"What's the plan, Darcy?"

"Are you busy tomorrow?"

Ryder shook his head.

"Good. Because now you are. Friendsgiving at my place."

Ryder grimaced. "I'd rather rent the damn limo."

"Nope. My family is a big part of who I am, and you've never really given them a chance. Besides, I think we need to work on that not-a-people-person problem of yours. You spend too much time on your own, and you need to do something fun with other people."

Ryder wanted to argue that what she considered an attempt to make him like people was the very definition of a trial by fire, but instead, he found himself nodding. It was as if he was completely incapable of denying her anything. "Fine. I'll come to Friendsgiving, but I plan the next date. And there won't be a limo."

"Deal."

She'd suggested dates that revealed what their lives were like. She already knew what his life was life, but she'd only been on the outer fringes, present when he was absent. He wanted her to see that he wasn't lying about the two most important things in his life—his job and his boys.

Then he realized there was another condition they needed to agree on.

"I don't think we should tell anyone we're dating. Since it's just a trial."

She tilted her head. "Okay. Can I ask why not?"

"Clint."

"Clint?" she asked.

"Darcy, the kid is crazy about you. I don't ever want to jeopardize your relationship with my son. He lost his mom when he was just seven years old. Since then, you and Yvonne have been there for him, giving him something Leo and I can't. Those tummy rubs and cuddles and the fussing over him. He needs that. He sees us as friends right now, and I think it's best if we keep it that way."

She nodded. "You're right. I get that. We should keep it just between us. But you should also know that whether this succeeds or fails, I'm never going to stop being there for Clint."

Ryder was touched by her love for his son. "Good."

Darcy held out her hand, her smile one of pure mischief. "So...should we shake on it? Or kiss? It is Friday after all."

He took her hand, not to shake but to pull her closer. Actually, there was still one more thing they needed to discuss, something that might very well be the deal breaker for her. "Maybe this would be a good time for me to give you a taste of what you're signing on for. Then, you can decide if you still want to go out with me."

"I do wan—"

"No," he interrupted. "Don't answer me until after."

"After?" she whispered.

"Lift your skirt and bend over my desk. Facedown."

Ryder stifled a groan when Darcy moved into the position he requested, without saying another word. She didn't hesitate, not even for a second.

Fuck. If she was genuinely submissive, he wasn't sure he'd ever find his way back.

He adjusted his pants, which were too tight, thanks to the erection that had emerged the second she'd walked into his office and locked the door.

She wore a bright red thong that was more suggestion than underwear, and Ryder cursed himself for starting this, knowing he couldn't finish. Not here.

He stepped behind her, running his hands over the soft, bare skin of her ass. Darcy shivered under his touch, the reaction reminding him that in this, she was an innocent.

"I need you to define unintentional virgin. How far have you gone?" he asked.

She lifted her head and twisted to look at him. "Making out. Heavy petting. I just never found the guy I wanted to," she paused, then grinned as she added, "seal the deal with."

"And on Halloween, in the elevator," he started. "You would have sealed the deal?"

"Yes," she whispered.

Ryder nodded. He'd known that. She was twenty-four, and she'd obviously had opportunities to sleep with other men. She'd refused them...but not *him*.

It was a gift she was offering, and a stronger, better man might refuse. He couldn't—wouldn't. He wanted her more than he'd ever wanted any woman, and he was just arrogant enough to know he could make her first time good for her.

Darcy deserved a man with experience, someone who would take his time and give her everything she wanted and more. The list she rattled off in the elevator floated through his mind.

Tied up. Held down. Spanked. Taken.

For her, right now, those were just words, ideas, and it was a far cry between fantasizing about something and doing it.

Regardless, Ryder wanted to be the man to give her all of that. The thought of her trying those things with anyone else had him seeing red.

He bent over her body, reaching up to where her hands were pressed flat against the top of his desk. He placed his hands on hers. "I'm going to hold you down, tie you up. Keep you in my bed, helpless to do anything but accept my will. Are you sure you can you handle that?"

Her breath was ragged as she whispered just one word. "Yes."

He kissed her cheek before releasing her hands and standing once more. He raised one hand and brought it down on her ass. Hard. The spot he spanked flushed pink.

"Ah!" she cried out quietly, just one airy, surprised, aroused breath. He couldn't wait to pull her over his lap and spank her for real, feel her wiggling beneath him. His fingers itched to do it properly, but he couldn't. Not now, not here, when there were too many people around to hear.

Soon.

"I'm going to pull you over my lap and spank you until you come, Darcy. I'm going to control your orgasms, your body, your pleasure, your pain. I'm not an easy lover. Are you sure that's what you want?"

"God... So much."

He tapped the inside of one of her ankles, silently instructing her to part her legs. As soon as she did, he pulled her thong aside and ran his finger along her slit, thrilled to discover her so wet, so hot, so ready.

"Ryder, please," she whispered.

"Do you own any toys?"

Her right cheek was pressed against his desk, which allowed him to see the blush that bloomed at his question. "I...um..."

"I'm going to take that as a yes."

She didn't look at him as she answered. "A vibrator. And a dildo."

"I'll use them on you, buy you more."

"Ryder... Please. I want it all. Want you. Now."

"No. Your first time isn't going to be over my desk any more than it was going to be on the floor of an elevator. You deserve better than that. When I take you, Darcy, it's going to be in a bed, and it's going to be all night."

He was an idiot to start this here, but he wasn't going to hide who he was, what he needed from her. He'd done that once before, shut down the part of him that needed control in the bedroom because Denise hadn't liked it.

Denise had pretended to enjoy his dominance, his rough touch, when they were dating, but a year or so after Clint was born, they'd been in the middle of a huge fight when she'd told him the things he did in the bedroom scared her. He'd been so blindsided, so upset to think he'd hurt or frightened her that he'd closed that part of himself down completely, and the two of them had never done anything more adventurous than missionary after that until their sex life died a slow, painful death.

"Darcy, if any of what I just said scares you, you have to—"

"Scares me?" She pressed upwards, and he gave way, needing to see her expression when she answered. Her skirt fell back into place as she turned to face him.

"None of that scares me. It turns me on more than I can express. I want you to teach me...all of it. And I don't want you to hold back because you're afraid of scaring me. Promise me you won't do that," she demanded.

"I won't do that." He cupped her face and kissed her again. They broke apart, both startled when the phone on his desk rang. "Shit." He looked at his watch. "I'm supposed to be in a meeting. I'm late. Again."

"That's okay. So...tomorrow?"

He nodded, trying not to acknowledge the fact tomorrow now felt like a lifetime away. "Tomorrow."

She turned to leave, but before she reached the door, he gripped her upper arm, pulling her back toward him, giving her one more long, deep kiss, aware he wasn't going to be able to concentrate in the upcoming meeting any better than he had in all the others since Halloween.

Because now he wasn't merely longing for her.

He was making plans. Plans he couldn't wait to carry out.

And for the first time in a long time, he was looking forward to the future.

CHAPTER EIGHT

"What are you doing here?" Darcy asked with a covert wink when Ryder followed Yvonne and Leo upstairs for Friendsgiving Saturday afternoon.

Darcy had been pretty proud of the secret trial-run dating idea. After Denise's betrayal, Ryder had convinced himself he didn't need or want another woman in his life, and she was determined to prove him wrong.

Yvonne grinned at Darcy. "Shocking, right? I invited Ryder to come along...like I *allllways* do," she drawled. "And he actually said yes this time. You could've knocked me over with a feather."

Ryder rolled his eyes. "Very funny, Vonnie. You know I don't always say no. I came to your birthday party last year."

"That was two years ago," Yvonne corrected. "And that was the last time."

Darcy laughed. "Well, the more the merrier because many hands make light work."

"How many clichés can you squeeze into one sentence?" Ryder teased.

Yvonne grasped Leo's hand and pulled him across the living room. "We're on kitchen duty. I have three pies to make and Leo is my apple peeler."

"Sunnie and Landon are already in there. And Ollie and Gavin are out running errands, so if you forgot anything, text them. Everyone else should be showing up soon," Darcy explained. "Ryder, you're with me. I need help setting up the tables."

Ryder feigned a sigh like he was put out as he followed Darcy up a second set of stairs. As soon as they were out of sight of the others, he reached out and playfully smacked her butt. "I like your ass," he murmured.

"Yours isn't so bad, either. Looks hot in those jeans." Darcy loved this newly discovered lighthearted side of Ryder. For years, she'd thought he was serious and stuffy. She couldn't have been more wrong.

"Where are we going?" he asked.

"We have some folding tables up here in storage. We pull them down for the holidays and special occasions."

"I'm surprised they ever get put away," he teased.

She peered over her shoulder and grinned as they passed two bedrooms on their way to what was clearly a "junk" room. "Colm has a bedroom up here, and my brother Finn used to as well, before he moved in with Layla and Miguel. The other two rooms are where we store all the...well, for lack of a better word...crap."

"I can see that," Ryder said, glancing around the room at more "crap" than he'd ever seen in his life. Though he had to admit, the Collins clan was very good at keeping their shit organized and accessible. There were several large shelves lining the walls with labeled boxes that contained everything from dishes to Christmas decorations to tools. Stacked and leaning against one wall were five long plastic, foldable banquet tables.

When he gave her a questioning glance at why they needed that many, Darcy had her response ready. "My family is fifty people strong when we all show up."

Ryder winced. "Jesus. Growing up, my family consisted of me, my mom, and my dad. And that was two people too many."

Darcy tilted her head and realized she didn't know much about Ryder's upbringing or his family. "You aren't close to your parents?"

He shook his head. "I haven't seen them in over a decade."

Darcy's eyes widened. "Oh my God. That's terrible. I talk to my mom and dad pretty much every day."

Ryder shrugged, and it was clear he didn't consider the lack of communication with his parents any big loss. "That's because your parents are cool, whereas mine are chilly. Totally different temperatures."

"Yeah, but—"

Ryder reached out and cupped her cheek. "Hey. This isn't a bad thing, honest. My family sucked, so I made my own. Got pretty lucky with Leo and Yvonne, the boys, and now Reba. I traded up, okay?"

She grinned. "You have an awesome family. I'm glad to hear you say that."

Ryder's hand was still on her face, and he used it to pull her closer. "Yeah. I've been walking around with blinders on.

I appreciate you pointing that out because I didn't realize how much I've been missing at home. Got Reba all to myself for a whole hour yesterday while Leo and Vonnie went grocery shopping."

Okay. Well, that did it for her. The fact that Ryder was grinning from ear to ear over getting to spend an hour with the baby pretty much ensured her heart was lost to him forever.

"That's awesome."

"So how many of these tables do we need?"

"Only a couple. This is a smaller party. Just my cousins, brother, sister, and friends. I think you'll know almost everyone. Emmy is coming with Paddy."

Ryder nodded. "She's the romance writer, right?"

"Yep. She's super sweet. I love her. My bestie, Brooklyn, is going to be here with her fellas, and Ollie's got a new girl, Erin. And a few other friends." She paused. "And I should warn you, before we eat, we all go around and name one person in the room we're thankful for and why. It's sort of a twist on Thanksgiving—where we list everything and everyone we're thankful for."

"You seriously do that every year at Thanksgiving? All fifty of you? How long does that take?"

Darcy laughed at his astonished tone. "It doesn't take that long, and we pass the bottle of Jameson as we go around, so by the end, believe me, no one has noticed the time."

Ryder rubbed his forehead as if he couldn't imagine anything worse.

"What do you do for Thanksgiving?" she asked.

"Clint and I go out to dinner. Try a different restaurant every year. Then we come home and watch football."

Darcy crinkled her nose. "You eat out? Please tell me you at least have turkey."

Ryder shrugged casually. "Sometimes but not always. Last year, we had Chinese."

"That doesn't sound like much of a holiday."

Ryder tapped her nose playfully. "Traditions are what you make them, Buttercup."

"I guess that's true. But...well...if you guys wanted, you could come to Thanksgiving here this year. Leo, Vonnie, Vince, and Reba are all coming."

Ryder smiled, but she could almost imagine the wheels spinning in his brain as he tried to think of an excuse. "Let's see how tonight goes before I commit to that."

She rolled her eyes. "You and your aversion to people."

"I don't think it's the people that bother me as much as big crowds and noise."

Darcy blew out a long sigh. "Well, then you're probably not going to like tonight. We're sort of a loud family."

"I'm aware."

"We all talk at the same time."

Ryder chuckled. "I've noticed that. Don't worry, Darc. I'm going into this with an open mind."

"Thanks."

Ryder gave her a quick kiss, and then they each grabbed the end of one of the tables. Ryder could have carried it himself, but she insisted on helping.

Within half an hour, they had the two extra tables, as well as the long dining room table, set for the meal. Everyone starting showing up over the course of the next hour. It was every bit as loud as she'd warned Ryder, but he was either being an extremely good sport or was genuinely enjoying himself.

Just before the meal, they did their annual "friend I'm most thankful for."

Darcy gave Ryder a teasing grin when it was his turn. She expected him to be thankful for Yvonne and Leo—so she was shocked when he pointed to her.

"I'm thankful for Darcy. She came into my life during a very difficult time for me, and for the past four years, she's always been there, no matter what I needed—help with the boys, a new graphic artist at work, or even just someone to explain what the hell is going on in Fortnite."

Everyone laughed, and Lochlan raised his beer bottle. "I feel you there, man."

Ryder continued, looking directly at her. "I've never once said thanks, Darcy, for all you've done for me, so I'm glad to get the chance now. I'm very thankful to have you in my and Clint's lives."

Darcy was so touched, she had to fight hard not to cry. She caught the far-too-interested gazes from her friends, Kelli and Brooklyn, who would no doubt corner her later to ask what was up. Then Sunnie gave her a knowing wink that made her blush as much as Ryder's kind words.

It was Darcy's turn next. "Well, this is kind of awkward. Because I was going to say I was thankful for Ryder for getting me a job with a 401K. Seems to pale in comparison."

Ryder laughed and reached out to ruffle her hair affectionately. They'd agreed to keep the trial run on the down low, but Ryder wasn't going out of his way to hide much. He'd spent most of the afternoon standing next to her, and he'd claimed the seat at the table beside her.

Typically, it wasn't unusual for Friendsgiving to run well into the wee hours of night, but this year was different. Caitlyn, who was pregnant, was suffering from what she called morning, noon, and night sickness, so she and her husband, Lucas, left right after dinner. Oliver and Gavin had seemed to be out of sorts all night, which was weird because they were usually thick as thieves. Darcy wasn't sure what was going on, but she wondered if it had something to do with the fact Ollie had a new girlfriend, Erin, and things between them seemed to be getting serious quick.

Even Colm, who was always ready to take things to the next level, was quieter than normal. When Kelli, the ultimate party girl, said she was going to call it an early night as well, Colm offered to walk her home, and Darcy knew that Friendsgiving was officially over.

Yvonne, as always, was anxious to get back to Reba. "Well, I can't believe you made it to the end," Yvonne teased Ryder before looking at Darcy. "He insisted on bringing his own car in case he wanted to leave early. Of course, this is wrapping up way earlier than usual."

Leo helped Yvonne put on her coat. "Everyone is still probably hungover from that Halloween party."

"You were planning to leave early?" Darcy joked with Ryder, pretending to be insulted that he had an escape route, when inside, her stomach was turning flip-flops at the thought he'd brought his own car. "How unlike you."

Even as she spoke, Darcy didn't dare look him directly in the eye.

She prayed he intended to stay...hopefully all night.

Her prayers seemed to be answered when Ryder said,

"I'm going to stick around a little while. Help Darcy put the tables back upstairs."

Yvonne smiled. "That's sweet of you. See you at home." She picked up the dessert plate they'd wrapped up for the boys and headed to the stairs that led down to the pub. Darcy caught the quick look Leo and Ryder exchanged, curious when Leo nodded his head, even though neither of them had spoken.

"What was that?" Darcy murmured.

Ryder just smiled and shrugged. They said their good-byes to Lochlan and May, who followed Yvonne and Leo out, and over the course of the next half hour, everyone else finished cleaning up and headed back to their own places.

Oliver, one of the last to leave, said he was going to drive Erin home, and Darcy suspected he would spend the night at her place. When it was just Darcy, Ryder, and Gavin left in the Collins Dorn, Gavin said he was going to head down to the pub to watch the hockey game and hang with Uncle Tris, who was manning the bar, for a little while.

"So?" she prompted, once Gavin was gone.

Ryder gave her a quizzical look. "So what?"

"What did you think of Friendsgiving? Of a Collins event?"

Ryder frowned, blowing out a long breath as she held hers. He'd said he didn't like people, crowds, or noise. Three things that were impossible to avoid in her family. Until that moment, Darcy hadn't really thought about what she might consider a relationship deal breaker, but as she looked at Ryder's serious expression, she realized she would struggle to be with a man who didn't like her family.

"Wellllll," he drawled. "I hate to say this to you, mainly

because I'm not the type to admit I was wrong easily...but they're great, Darc. I mean, I've met them, known them, liked them all for years, but most of those interactions were one-on-one whenever I ran into them on the street or in the pub. I'm not sure why I was so determined to avoid the big gatherings. Tonight was a lot of fun. They're easy to be around. You're really lucky, blessed with your family."

She hugged him, so delighted by everything he said. "I know I am. They mean everything to me."

Then...something occurred to her and she looked around, frowning.

"What's wrong?" he asked.

She'd been so worried about Ryder's feelings about her family, she hadn't put two and two together. "We're alone in the dorm. You realize that never happens, right?"

Ryder grinned as he stepped closer to her, placing his hands on her waist. "Buttercup," he said.

"Yeah?"

"Where's your bedroom?"

She took his hand and led him down the hallway to her room on the end. It was the largest room in the apartment and had been shared by her mother and aunts Keira and Teagan growing up. As soon as they were inside, Ryder closed the door, locked it, then leaned against it.

"Darcy—" he started.

She knew what he was going to say the second he opened his mouth, so she cut him off at the pass. "I'm sure, Ryder. I've never wanted anything more in my life."

For a moment, he looked as if all the air in his body had slowly seeped out, and she realized how tense he'd been. "I want you too. More than I can say."

He pushed away from the door and walked toward her. She met him halfway, their lips touching as he wrapped his arms around her waist, hers looping over his shoulders. Their tongues tangled, his breath sweet from the apple pie, bitter from the coffee. It was as if she was getting her dessert twice.

They remained there, content to kiss, to explore, to caress. Ryder wasn't rushing her, wasn't attempting to push her too fast.

She appreciated that.

Until she didn't.

Darcy wanted—needed—skin to skin, his body on top of hers, inside hers.

"Please," she whispered after several minutes, twisting her head to suck in some much-needed air.

Ryder gripped the back of her neck with one large, strong hand, forcing her passion-drunk eyes to focus on him. "Those things I said in my office yesterday...the things I want to do to you..."

She nodded, letting him know she knew exactly what he was referring to. God. It was all she could think about last night as she'd tossed and turned and fantasized and masturbated her way through two orgasms.

"Not tonight," he said.

She frowned, her shock giving way to panic.

No. No fucking way.

She was too ready for this, and if he seriously tried to leave her here, still a damn virgin, she'd bar the door and do the tying up herself.

"Ryder, please. Don't—"

He kissed her, this touch rougher, more possessive. He was using the kiss to stop her from talking.

It was effective.

Dammit.

"It's your first time, Darcy. No games tonight. Just you and me. Do you understand?"

Darcy swallowed the lump in her throat, fighting tears. Every freaking thing he'd said tonight had seriously moved her to tears. Beautiful tears.

"Darcy. Tell me you understand."

She nodded. "I do. I want that too."

"Are you on birth control?"

Her cheeks suddenly felt warm and she was certain she was blushing. "Yes. The pill."

He paused for a moment as if considering her answer. "And you take them? Faithfully?"

She nodded. "Every morning."

Ryder didn't move, and she fought to understand the sudden...well, she couldn't tell what she was seeing on his face. It could have been confusion or anxiety or...even anger.

She hated all of them. "I know where Colm hides his emergency stash of condoms." She pointed to her bedroom door. "They're just down the hall in the bathroom. I can run down and grab—"

"No," he interjected. "I...don't want anything between us."

His words made her happy, and she would have smiled, but the sweetness of what he was saying didn't match the expression or the tone.

"Ryder—" she started, clueless as to what was going through his brain.

Before she could attempt any sort of reassurance, the fog lifted and she fought for breath as Ryder obviously shook off whatever was bothering him and gave her a smile that was pure seduction.

Then he took a step away, reached for the hem of her sweater, and pulled it off.

"Time to take care of our similar problems," he said.

CHAPTER NINE

Ryder ran his fingers along the top of Darcy's bra, certain he'd never seen a more beautiful woman. He'd spent the entire afternoon half-erect, fighting the overwhelming desire to drag Darcy away from the party—family be damned—strip her naked, and lose himself inside her.

He knew he was being a fool to forgo the condom, but there were two fundamental truths that outweighed all of his fears.

One, Darcy wasn't Denise, and while he struggled with trust, there was a persistent voice inside that told him he could trust her, that he *did* trust her.

And two, apparently, he was a fucking caveman.

He wanted to come inside her, mark her as his own. It was a new emotion for him, but damn if it wasn't a powerful one. He'd never wanted to possess a woman, claim her.

But as he looked at Darcy in her bra, her cheeks flushed with arousal and maybe a little bit of embarrassment, it was all he could do not to beat his chest, toss her over his shoulder, and drag her to his cave.

Darcy began to unbutton his shirt, her fingers trembling slightly as she slipped each one free. Throughout, her eyes never left his. He recalled her doing the same thing in the elevator the night of Halloween...and that night so many years ago.

Once his shirt was open, her gaze drifted lower as she ran her hand over his chest. Ryder reached around her and unhooked her bra, drawing the straps over her shoulders.

"You're so beautiful," he murmured.

She smiled shyly. "So are you."

Ryder bent his head to kiss her again, unable to resist the feeling of his lips against hers. As they kissed, he pushed her backwards, one slow step at a time, until they reached her bed. Her bedroom was larger than he would have expected, and mercifully, she had a double bed, not a single.

Ryder unfastened her jeans, drawing the zipper down. They worked together to tug down the tight denim as well as her panties. She'd been barefoot all day, not bothering with shoes in her own house.

Once she was completely naked, he took a step back so he could look at her. Darcy, though inexperienced, possessed a confidence he found captivating, attractive. She'd been raised in the midst of a loving family, who'd instilled in her a strong sense of self-worth.

"Lay down on the bed, Buttercup."

She sank onto the mattress, scooting to the middle, leaning back and supporting her weight with her hands behind her.

He shook his head. "Lay down," he repeated, perfectly

aware he was pushing her. He was still essentially dressed, only his shirt hanging open, while she was completely naked. Lying down while he stood would make her feel even more vulnerable, but Ryder wanted her to know she never needed to feel that way with him.

She dropped down, her long hair flowing over the pillow beneath her head, framing her heart-shaped face like a dark-chocolate halo. Her bright blue eyes never left his face and he felt as though he could see straight to her soul through them. Darcy was so open, so guileless, able to express her emotions so freely. He could see her excitement, her desire, her happiness.

"So fucking beautiful," he repeated, smiling.

"Ryder," she whispered when he sat on the edge of the bed next to her. "What about your cloth—"

"I'm not rushing through a single second of this, Darcy. It'll be hard enough for me to hold back once I'm inside you. It's been too long...and God, I want you so bad."

She tried to sit up once more, but he pressed her down with a firm hand on her shoulder. "Lie still."

Ryder toed off his shoes, then shifted, crawling over her until she was caged beneath him. He kissed her again, taking his time with her lips, before moving on, exploring her cheeks, the sensitive spot behind her ear that produced the cutest little squeak when he licked it. Then he kissed her down along her throat, licking a path all the way to her breasts.

Her chest was rising and falling, her breathing acceler-ated, her entire body flushed with arousal. He lowered his head and took one of her rosy nipples into his mouth, sucking on the tight nub as Darcy began to wiggle, her hips lifting from the bed.

He took his time with her breasts, using his mouth and fingers, toying with her nipples, squeezing them, cupping them.

Darcy's head twisted from side to side, her eyes closed, her hands fisted in his hair. She'd begun to whisper her pleas for more, for everything.

Ryder lifted his head briefly and shrugged off his shirt, tossing it to the floor by the bed. Darcy's eyes opened, her fingers tracing his muscles, his nipples. She unbuttoned his jeans as he watched, then slowly slid the zipper down.

Ryder held his breath, praying he'd find the strength to hold on. It had been too many years, and she was too perfect.

Her fingers accidentally brushed the head of his dick as she lowered the zipper, and he hissed, pulled away. She frowned, obviously thinking she'd hurt him.

He shook his head. "You can't touch me. Not this first time. Jesus. Maybe not the first twenty times. It's been too long," he admitted.

"Twenty times," she repeated, grinning, even as she nodded her understanding, unresisting when he grasped her wrists and raised them to the pillow under her head. He pressed them firmly for just a moment.

"Keep your hands there. Just like that," he murmured deeply. "Surrender to me, Darcy."

She trembled but not in fear. "Yes," she whispered.

God. He was suddenly sorry he'd taken bondage off the table for tonight. Darcy's desires hadn't been born out of an innocent woman's curiosity. She was truly submissive, her easy acquiescence drawing out his dominant side.

He didn't remove his jeans. Not yet. He couldn't. The second he released the beast, there was no way he could stop himself from taking her.

And he wouldn't do that until she came first.

Ryder slid down, pushing her legs farther apart.

"Oh God," Darcy whispered shakily.

Ryder smiled, aware she couldn't see the response her words prompted. He licked her, one long stroke of his tongue along her slit as she trembled harder.

"So good. It's all so good," she said, her words so Darcy. She wouldn't hold back anything, not her responses, her words, her feelings.

Ryder placed his thumb against her clit as he licked her again, applying pressure, wiggling it, and Darcy jerked as if struck by lightning.

"Omigod. There!" she said, as if he couldn't tell he'd struck gold for himself. "Right there."

He continued to move his thumb, varying the pressure and the speed until he knew she was getting close. With his other hand, he slid two fingers inside her wet, tight heat. Darcy's back arched and she cried out loudly.

"Holy shit! Yes!"

He was glad they were alone in the apartment because there was no way her cousins wouldn't know what was going on after that. He'd only stroked in and out of her pussy half a dozen times, his thumb still playing with her clit, when she came. Hard.

For a split second, her heavy breathing halted as her eyes squeezed shut tight, her inner muscles contracting against his fingers.

"Fuck," she moaned, as he started moving his fingers

again, determined to draw out her orgasm. Watching Darcy come was about to become his favorite pastime. There was no way he'd be able to resist driving her to climax again and again and again.

She started to come down, slowly, her body shaking slightly. Ryder wanted more. He wanted a hell of a lot more. He curled his fingers, searching.

Darcy's hands flew up, as did her upper body, stiffening when he found her G-spot.

"Ryder!" she yelled, just before she fell over the edge again, coming once more. She dropped back to the bed when it started to wane, whimpering slightly when he pulled his fingers out.

"Did I hurt you?"

She shook her head. "Only in the best possible way. I thought I was going to die."

He grinned, moving upwards so that he could kiss her. He'd never kissed a woman this much in bed. Typically the kisses were a prelude, something he'd spend a few minutes doing before moving on to the main act.

With Darcy, kissing was different. Less foreplay and more necessity. He craved the act, needed the emotional closeness he felt with his lips pressed to hers, the heat of her breath against his face, the sweet smile she gave him every time they parted, and the way her eyes looked at him as if he was the most important man in her life.

It was heady. Addictive. And maybe tomorrow, when lust wasn't coursing through his brain, clogging up the works and rendering him stupid, he might worry about all of that.

Right now, he needed her kisses more than air.

Darcy's hands stroked his shoulders, his bare back, and

he realized she was suffering from the need to touch him as well.

"Inside me," she whispered after several minutes. "Please. I need you so bad."

Ryder sluggishly pushed himself up until he was standing by the bed. He felt drunk, trashed, wasted, and he hadn't had a drop of alcohol.

Shoving his jeans and boxers down, he kicked them and his socks off as Darcy shifted to her side, propped herself up on her elbow, her gaze missing nothing. She studied his cock intently, not with fear or intimidation, but genuine interest and appreciation.

"Darcy," he started. Once he got back in the bed, he wasn't sure he trusted himself to stop. His desire for her was off the charts.

She shook her head. "I'm not scared, and I don't want to stop."

He wondered if she could read minds. Then it occurred to him that perhaps she wasn't the only one wearing her heart on her sleeve, speaking volumes with her eyes. He'd never been with a woman who could read him so well, who could understand his feelings, his fears, without him having to say a single word.

She lay back down and lifted her arms in invitation. Ryder lowered himself to the bed, on top of her. Her legs were parted, cradling his hips between them. His cock lay nestled in the warmth of her slit, her arousal coating his hard flesh. She'd been tight around just two of his fingers. His cock was thicker.

"You said you have toys," Ryder said, suddenly worried about genuinely hurting her. He'd never slept with a virgin.

She nodded. "I'm sure there's nothing there," she paused, blushing, "to break. But..." Her eyes lowered, and for the first time since she'd invited him to her room, he sensed she was truly embarrassed.

"But what?"

"Well, my toys aren't as big as..." She glanced up and made the cutest little face, her eyes wide as she gave him a crooked grin.

Ryder couldn't help it. He laughed. "God, Darcy. You're..." He struggled for a word, nothing seeming right. Finally, he landed on, "Perfect."

He kissed her again. Because how could he not?

Darcy slowly started tilting her hips, rubbing herself on his cock until Ryder feared he'd come before he ever made it inside.

"I'm afraid this won't last long," he admitted.

She caressed his cheek. "For me, either. Besides...I'm hoping we're going to do this more than just once tonight. Twenty times, I think you said."

He kissed her throat, his lips sliding up to her ear. "Let's wait until after to decide that. I don't want to hurt you."

Ryder lifted his hips, reaching down to direct his dick toward her opening. He pressed in slowly, stopping when just the head was inside.

"Don't stop," she whispered, and too many powerful, positive emotions swamped him as he suddenly realized he and Darcy had been hurtling headfirst toward this moment for years.

He pushed deeper, not stopping until he was fully lodged. He paused, not so much for her but for him.

Jesus. Christ. She was tight. *Very* tight. And hot. And wet.

And he was suddenly missing the blood that should have been pumping through his brain because if there was a drop there, he might have found a way to distract himself, to make this last longer than a second or three.

"Fuck," he muttered when Darcy tilted her hips, driving him the tiniest bit deeper. Even that slight motion was more than he could handle.

"Don't move," he said, sucking in as much air as he could. "Just give me a second to…"

"Look at me, Ryder," Darcy said. "Do it. Hard. Fast. I promise I'll be right there with you. And then we're going to do it again. And again."

He didn't respond. He couldn't. She'd set him free.

Ryder withdrew, gritting his teeth so hard, he feared he'd crack them. He reached for her clit, stroked it, the touch provoking the response he knew would ring the death knell for him.

She jerked upwards and, after that, it was a fifty-yard dash to the finish line. Ryder thrust hard and fast, over and over, as Darcy met him blow for blow.

His intention had been finesse, gentleness, care.

Instead, he was fucking her like it was his last night on Earth, taking her with a need so powerful, it made him dizzy.

Darcy cried out his name, scratched his back and, less than a minute later, she came, pulsing tightly around his dick as his climax crashed down on him.

He called out her name repeatedly as he spilled every single of drop of come deep inside her body. Darcy trembled as she wrapped her arms around him, holding him tightly, his chest to her breasts.

As his wits began to return, he realized he was probably crushing her beneath his weight, but Darcy didn't complain or even loosen her grip, determined to keep him on her, close to her.

Finally, he managed to find the strength to shove himself to the side. Darcy twisted with him so that when he landed on his back, she was there, curling into his embrace like a sleepy kitten.

He placed several kisses to the top of her head, whispering her name, telling her she was amazing, beautiful, perfect. Everything.

She was everything to him.

Ryder didn't know how much she'd heard before her breathing had steadied, the slow, gentle inhalations and exhalations telling him she'd fallen asleep.

He was physically exhausted, but emotionally, it was as if he'd taken a hit of speed. His previously sluggish brain was suddenly alert and focused and aware of just one thing.

They were only one date in, and he was already in way too deep. With that thought, his throat began to close, his chest tightening, as wave after wave of panic washed through him. He couldn't do this again. Couldn't go through it all again.

Memories of the past four years crashed over him—the betrayal, the pain, the loneliness.

Losing Denise had taken him down hard.

Losing Darcy?

Fuck.

That would finish him off for good.

CHAPTER TEN

Darcy stared at her computer screen and realized she hadn't done a single thing to the flyer she was working on in the past twenty minutes. Her thoughts were consumed with Ryder.

She'd fallen asleep in his arms Saturday night after losing her virginity. She was pretty sure that in the history of "deflowerings," hers had been the best ever. Ryder had been so incredibly sweet and careful and sexy.

She'd replayed it at least a million times since then, and it had only been thirty-six hours.

She had hoped to expand on the experience, but Ryder had been up and dressed early Sunday morning when she woke. He'd been waiting for her, sitting on the edge of the bed, watching her sleep. Everything about it had felt so romantic.

She'd tried to convince him to take his clothes off and come back to bed, but he'd said he wanted to be home before Clint woke up and realized he hadn't been home all night.

She understood and respected that, even though she was disappointed. They'd only had sex once and that hadn't been anywhere near enough for her.

Not just because it had been amazing, as in top-three-orgasms-of-her-life amazing, but because it had only whetted her appetite for more.

It had been on the tip of her tongue to invite him and Clint to watch football with her and her cousins yesterday, but before she could say anything, Ryder had mentioned having a lot of chores to do. He'd kissed her—not as passionately as he had the night before, but still pretty damn decently—and then said he'd see her at work on Monday.

She had texted him a couple times yesterday, but his responses—though perfectly fine—had taken a long time coming. When it became somewhat obvious he either didn't have time to text or didn't want to—she prayed it wasn't the latter—she had stopped, deciding she'd let him take the lead on communicating with her.

He hadn't initiated anything after that. No texts and no calls from him.

Darcy was fighting like hell not to read too much into that, desperate not to become one of those women who fell apart if a guy wasn't talking to her every second of the day, but there'd been something—something she couldn't put her finger on—in Ryder's face Sunday morning that was bothering her.

So here she was at work...at noon on Monday...and she still hadn't seen Ryder. The door to his office had been closed all morning, which was unusual. He rarely worked with it closed, unless he was in a meeting.

She sighed and decided fuck it, hitting the save button on her project, not that she'd done much to save. She really did have a substantial to-do list for work, but until she saw Ryder, until she could push aside this uneasiness that maybe things hadn't been as great for him, she'd never accomplish a damn thing.

Darcy was about to go knock on his door, certain she was simply letting her imagination run away from her, when the phone on her desk rang. Ryder's name popped up, and she breathed a sigh of relief, silently chastising herself for acting like a silly teenage girl.

"See. You're an idiot," she muttered to herself before answering the phone.

"Hello, Ryder," she said.

"Can you come to my office, Darcy?"

"Sure. Of course."

"Thanks."

His tone sounded fine, but that nagging unease in the back of her brain was rattling again.

She stood up, trying to press the wrinkles in her skirt away with her hand. Then she walked to his office. The door was still closed, so she knocked.

"Come in."

She opened the door and entered, pausing just over the threshold.

"Close it," Ryder said. "And lock it."

She did as he said, fighting not to smile. The last time he'd told her to lock the door, he'd bent her over his desk and rattled off the sexiest list of things he wanted to do to her that she'd ever heard.

And it had been *her* list!

It was just so much hotter coming from him…show-and-tell style.

She crossed the room, not stopping until she was standing next to him, behind his desk. "Busy morning?" she asked.

Ryder nodded slowly, but she could tell he was lying.

She hadn't imagined a thing. She'd spent three weeks trying to crash through the barrier Ryder insisted on putting up between them. It had fallen down Saturday, but damn if he hadn't rebuilt it since then.

"What's up?" she asked.

Ryder had been sitting in his desk chair, but at her question, he rose and took a step away. And then another. Until she was behind his desk and he was in front of it.

"I don't think we should continue dating."

Wow. Hello, Mr. Abrupt.

"Why not?" Darcy was fighting to appear strong, unaffected, but even she could hear the disappointment in her voice.

The look on Ryder's face told her he'd heard it too.

"I'm ten years older than you, Darcy."

"Oh my God. No. Just *no!*" she said, throwing up her hands. "I thought we'd made it over the lame-excuses hurdles. But hey, you know what? I'll humor you. I don't see how age matters."

"It does matter. Because you haven't experienced as much as I have. You're in a completely different place, different stage, of your life. You told me what you want from a relationship in that elevator, and I can promise you, I'm not that guy."

Darcy shook her head. "I didn't say anything about relationships that night. I described an ideal date, Ryder. And I'm old enough to know life and love aren't always sunshine and roses and *The Princess Bride*."

Ryder leaned forward, his palms flat against his desk. "I'm not saying you always look at the world through rose-colored glasses, but you mentioned your parents, and Yvonne and Leo, and I know exactly what it is you're looking for in a relationship. And trust me, there are men out there who can give you that. I'm not one of them."

Darcy couldn't make Ryder's words match the man he'd revealed to her Saturday night in her bedroom. As far as she could see, he was exactly what she'd described, what she dreamed of. "I don't understand why you think that."

"I'm not a romantic guy, Darcy. Nowhere near your Westley. Hell, I might be closer to that other guy, the prince."

"You think you're Humperdinck?" she asked, trying not to laugh. This conversation was insane.

"Yeah. But without that stupid-ass name."

She shook her head. "You're wrong."

"No. I'm not. I've done the marriage thing before. And I sucked at it. The same way my parents sucked at it. I'm the guy who will always forget your birthday or our anniversary. I say I'll be home for dinner at six, then roll in at nine. I can sleep through a baby crying in the middle of the night, and I'll never notice when you get a haircut. I know that because...I lived it. With Denise."

Darcy listened to his arguments, really listened, and realized there was something Ryder didn't understand. Because he had it all wrong. "Ryder...did you love Denise?"

"Fuck, Darcy," he muttered.

"It's a simple question. Yes or no?"

Ryder ran his hand through his hair and closed his eyes, as if by doing so, he could block out her and her question. Then, slowly, he opened them and locked gazes with her. "What is this power you have?" he asked, though she was pretty sure he was directing those words at himself. "What did you call it? A curse?"

She nodded, though she'd never explained her reason for calling it that to him. Because the truth was, it wasn't a curse like Ryder was probably thinking. Her cousin, Colm, declared the entire Collins family suffered from a curse where they all fell in love, fast and hard and forever. And none of them were exempt from it.

When they met their true loves, that was it. Game over.

She'd been struck by the curse when she was just twenty.

"You said it was a spell," she said, trying to distract him from the curse idea. There was no way in hell Ryder was ready to hear those three little words from her. They were written on her heart, but they would have to remain her secret for now.

"I don't seem to be capable of shielding a goddamn thing from you. You ask a question and suddenly I'm baring my soul."

She smiled, though her pleased response clearly tweaked his temper, and his eyes narrowed.

"And yet you still haven't answered my question. Did you love Denise?"

"Yeah. I did. But I couldn't make her happy. And I can't make you happy, either."

"But you do," she insisted.

He refused to acknowledge that. "Stick around a little while and I'll show you how wrong you are."

She frowned. "I'm not wrong."

"I think part of the reason I'm no longer in that dark place I told you about is because I stopped blaming Denise for all our misery. I told myself I was angry and hurt because she betrayed me, broke my heart. I consoled myself by calling her a faithless bitch. She left me for that other guy. But we were both to blame for our failed marriage. I was cold and distant, and I thought I could fix everything simply by making more money. Fruit didn't fall far from the tree," he said, grimacing.

"Don't you think if you married again, married someone you—" She stopped herself just short of saying *loved*, fairly certain that word would freak him out. "Cared for, that all those descriptions of your first marriage would be different because now you know better?"

He shook his head.

"No?" she asked.

"I don't know, but I have no intention of putting that theory to the test. I can't...I never want to hurt you, Darcy."

She was touched by his admission, even though the idea of him trying to walk away killed her. Everything that happened between them Saturday night belied his words, even though he refused to see that.

"Can I ask you another question?"

He blew out a hard breath, and she could tell he wanted to reject her request. He'd just admitted he was incapable of hiding things from her. But that wasn't completely true. Because there was something she still didn't understand.

"What is it?"

"Why haven't you been with a woman since Denise died? I can't believe there haven't been opportunities. And even if you aren't looking for a relationship, I'm sure there have been other women you've been interested in sexually."

He studied her face for a long, silent minute, and she wondered if this time she'd pushed too far.

Especially when Ryder walked away from her to the small seating area set up in the corner. Dropping down onto the leather couch, he patted the cushion next to him. Even as she crossed the room toward him, she could almost see his internal debate, could tell he was trying to decide if he was really going to answer. She sat next to him.

"After Denise died," he swallowed heavily, "I found it... difficult to..." He ran his hand through his hair. "I was impotent. I couldn't get an erection."

Darcy didn't respond immediately, shocked and confused. "But..."

"But that problem ended that night in the elevator."

"So..."

"So you can imagine my surprise. You seem to have a rather powerful effect on me."

"Just me?" she asked, still astonished by his confession.

He nodded. "Just you."

"I'm glad you told me. But doesn't that sort of prove we shouldn't stop what's happening between us."

"Darcy, please try to understand. It's not a road I'm willing to travel again. I'm not...good at it."

"I disagree."

Ryder shook his head slowly, but it felt like she was starting to wear him down.

At least until he grasped at his next straw. "It doesn't

matter. Because truthfully, me calling a halt has very little to do with my feelings for Denise."

Darcy frowned. "I don't understand."

"Saturday night...what we did...it wasn't...*me.*" Ryder reached out and grasped her wrist. She thought he'd been aiming for her hand, so she tried to move to take it.

Ryder didn't release her wrist. Instead, he tightened his hold. Given the way her body was reacting to his firm grip on her wrist, it was safe to say this was another area where they were well-suited. Her nipples budded, something that didn't escape Ryder's notice as his gaze drifted lower.

What he couldn't see was the way her pussy was clenching, her panties wet.

This argument was worse than the previous one, which made her think perhaps there was something else driving him, something he wasn't saying.

"Tell me what you want," she whispered.

His brows furrowed, though she couldn't tell if he was angry or frustrated or fighting the same heart-thumping, blood-pumping arousal she was.

"I'm not an easy lover."

"I didn't ask for easy," she said. "Actually, I'm pretty sure I asked for exactly the opposite."

He growled, the deep, guttural sound rumbling in his throat. He'd been the epitome of the gentle lover on Saturday, and while she'd loved every single moment of it, she would never be satisfied with just that.

"I'll make demands," he said harshly. "And I'll exp—"

"Demand something," she interjected. "Right now. What do you want?"

He didn't miss a beat. "You, on your knees."

Darcy shifted, leaving the couch, dropping down in front of him, her eyes locked with his.

"Fuck. This isn't...I'm trying... Get up, Darcy," he muttered, his jaw clenched tightly. He ran a hand through his chestnut-colored hair in frustration, clearly wrestling some serious demons.

"No."

His tone was pure exasperation when he said, "You gotta let me win one of these damn arguments."

She didn't mean to—and it certainly didn't help his disposition—but she laughed as he reached for her upper arms, intent on lifting her up. She held her ground, refusing to rise. "No. I don't."

"Dammit, I mean it."

She shook him off. "What else?" she asked. "What else do you want, Ryder? Tell me."

Ryder stared at her as she remained on the floor at his feet, his expression hard, but she knew his anger wasn't directed at her. It was directed at himself. He'd brought her in here with the intention of breaking things off. But there was no way in hell she was going down without a fight.

Her heart was racing, not out of fear, but excitement. This...this was what she'd wanted, what she'd hoped for from the beginning. If only she could make him loosen the noose he'd draped around his own neck and set himself free. She didn't doubt for a moment she'd go wild in his embrace.

"Cursed," he muttered.

This time, she knew better than to laugh or smile or even react. Though he had no clue what that word did to her. How it made her feel.

He unfastened his belt, his eyes never leaving hers. He

didn't say a word as he unzipped his pants, lifted his ass, and slid them and his boxers to his ankles.

Darcy's gaze slid down as she licked her lips, but she didn't move. He hadn't told her to. This was a test, and there was no way in hell Darcy was going to fail.

"Fuck," he muttered at last. Then he reached out and gripped her chin, drawing her eyes up to his. "I don't remember blowjobs on your list of prior experience."

She wasn't about to back down. She wanted this. Him. God, she wanted everything. "Then you'd better make those demands very specific."

"Open your mouth."

This time, Darcy gave him just the barest hint of a smile, and his eyes narrowed briefly in response. He was struggling with what was happening, so she schooled her features. After all, she wasn't the type to kick a dog when he was down.

Not that Ryder was down.

As she leaned forward, all she could see was how very, very *up* he was.

She opened her mouth when she was a mere inch from his dick.

"Lick my cock," he said, his voice deep, either with arousal or anger. She didn't know which and she definitely didn't care. "From base to tip. Don't stop until I tell you."

Darcy rested her hands on his upper thighs, outstretched just for her. She did as he commanded, licking her first dick.

She'd always thought blowjobs were for the guy, something a girl did for a man she cared about. Which was why Darcy had never done this before.

What she hadn't expected was to be so completely

turned on herself. She stroked him with the flat of her tongue, up and down, as he'd said, several times before she got bolder. Ryder groaned when she twirled the tip of her tongue around the head of his dick, stroking it across the small slit, tasting his precum.

Ryder's hands, which had rested on the couch cushion, flew up at her action, gripping her face between his large palms. "Do that again," he said gruffly.

She repeated the movement, twirling around three times before adding the stroke that seemed to have the same effect as him curling his fingers inside her pussy and finding her G-spot.

Ryder's fingers found their way into her hair and he used his grip there to guide her mouth lower. "Take me in your mouth."

He didn't have to ask twice.

Hell, he hadn't had to ask the first time. It had taken a great deal of self-control to hold back, to wait for his commands.

Ryder was well-endowed, filling her mouth in a way that was almost uncomfortable.

"Relax," he said, his voice softer as he stroked the side of her face. "You can do this. Take more."

She shifted, but before she could follow his directive, he gripped the back of her neck and pressed her downward, the head of his cock brushing the back of her throat.

"Jesus," he murmured to himself. "So long. It's... just...been...so..."

His heartbreaking words, the almost reverent tone, triggered something inside her. Her love for him was never in question, but she was shocked to discover how much more of her heart was still left for him to claim. Every moment she spent with him, she found herself losing more and more of it to him.

"Grip the base of my dick," he said. "Wrap your hand around it tightly."

Once again, she did as he said. With the addition of his hand and his cock buried deep in her mouth, she began to move in earnest.

Well, Ryder began to move her in earnest, was actually probably a more accurate statement. He resumed his grip in her hair and he used it to move her up and down along his hard flesh, taking her mouth.

Darcy tried to increase the speed, tried to take him deeper, but he was driving the car, holding the reins, and even though he was clearly enthralled by the blowjob and quickly approaching his climax, Ryder wasn't letting go, wasn't losing control.

In a last-ditch attempt, she reached lower, cupping his balls with her free hand.

Ryder hissed, his fists closing tighter around her hair, pulling it until her scalp stung. The slight twinge of pain sent electrical sparks through her body, her pussy clenching, empty, needy.

If she'd been able to speak, she would have snapped at him, would have demanded that he fuck her mouth the way she knew he wanted to. He was still holding back—and she hated it.

She closed her hand around his balls, trying to force his hand, searching for some way to make him as mindless as he always managed to make her.

Her attempts failed when he pushed her face away, his dick escaping her mouth with a pop. His eyes were blazing.

"Ryder—" she started.

"Not a word."

He shifted then, pressing on her shoulders until she lay on her back on the floor. He lifted her skirt and shoved the lace of her panties aside. With one stroke of his fingers along her slit, he got the answer to his unspoken question. She was wet. Ready.

Placing the head of his cock at her entrance, he paused. "Pill this morning?"

She'd only managed to nod her head once before he slammed inside, one long, hard, brutal stroke.

Darcy winced, even as she felt the first twinges of her orgasm start to fire.

He took her roughly, quickly. The office floor, with its thin carpet, was hard against her back, but she didn't care.

"Trying to take control?" he asked gruffly as he continued to pound inside her.

She shook her head, even though it was a lie. That was exactly what she'd tried to do. However, speech was beyond her as her inner muscles began to clench, white spots blinding her when her orgasm struck.

Ryder gritted his teeth. "Fuck. Dammit, Darcy." Her climax triggered his, and he came inside her, both of them gasping and groaning quietly, still aware of their surroundings, of their colleagues just outside the locked door.

Finesse and longevity were things they were going to have to work up to. Between her inexperience and his long dry spell, it was safe to say it was going to take some time before they could come together without this instant spontaneous combustion.

Ryder held himself above her, supporting his weight on his elbows for several long minutes before he was able to rise. She watched as he stood, wishing she could find the strength to do the same. He pulled his pants up and refastened them, his gaze locked on her as she lay at his feet like a sack of potatoes.

She wasn't sure what she'd accomplished, but his eyes were shuttered again, confused, still angry.

Darcy couldn't decide if she'd taken one step forward or three very large ones back.

Ryder wasn't finished fighting.

Which meant she wasn't, either.

She started to push herself up, but he shook his head.

"Stay there. Don't move." He walked to the small bathroom in his office and she heard water running.

As far as his demands went, remaining motionless was the easiest one to follow. Her bones felt like they'd turned to Jell-O, her pussy twinging. Her second time, though quicker and harder, had been even better than her first. And she knew they'd only scratched the surface of the things Ryder could teach her.

Ryder returned with a washcloth, and heat suffused her face when he ran it gently between her legs, wiping away the remnants of her arousal and his come.

"You're a shitty sub," he said, his voice deadpan, no heat behind the words.

She laughed, and this time, her response provoked a grin from him.

"We'll get there," she said softly.

He sighed, then tossed the washcloth aside, grasping her hand and helping her stand.

The two of them resumed their previous spots on the couch.

"Darcy—" he started.

"This isn't over."

He sighed and she held her breath, waited for him to dig out some other stupid reason for stopping.

"Okay," he said at last.

Darcy was surprised by his easy capitulation. "Okay?"

"If I continued to say no, would you stop nagging?"

She crossed her arms. "I don't nag."

He grinned. "That's another word for tenacious, so yes, you do. But for the sake of argument, I'll reword. Would you stop insisting?"

"Never," she replied. "You haven't given this a fair shot."

"So my answer remains the same. Okay. We'll go out on another date. And then this is over. Sunday after next. Ravens game. You, me, and the boys."

Darcy was surprised by his choice but by no means disappointed. Like her, he was taking this trial run seriously. His feelings about her family had mattered deeply to her, and it was clear he was running a similar test. "Okay. Sounds fun."

"I know how you are with the boys, Darcy. They love you. I just...you've never really seen *me* with them for extended periods of time."

"Ryder. I've seen you with them enough to know you're an amazing dad."

"Yeah, well, the game felt like a good trial. The boys mean everything to me."

"I can't wait."

"Today wasn't... We didn't accomplish... You still don't know—"

She placed her fingers against his lips. "I'm not scared. And I want more. Want it all. It's a marathon, not a sprint."

"You're wrong. It's a sprint. I'm going to show you exactly what kind of man I am. There won't be any holding back."

"Good," she said.

He scowled at her response. "And then this *will be* over."

She shook her head. "Nope."

"Yes. You'll see." He released her, his tone dismissive, self-assured.

If Darcy had one failing, it was that in arguments, she always had to get the last word. She could tell Ryder wasn't telling her the truth about why he was pushing her away. She wasn't sure how she knew, but there was something deep inside telling her that everything he'd said about her being too inexperienced, too young to handle what he wanted was a lie.

Of course, regardless of whether he believed that or not, she couldn't wait to prove him wrong.

She kissed him softly. "No, Ryder. It's *your* eyes that are going to be opened."

CHAPTER ELEVEN

Ryder stepped out of the kitchen and tossed the dishtowel over his shoulder when he heard a knock at the door. He'd been washing the few dishes left in the sink over the course of the day and then he was heating up some soup for Clint's dinner.

The two of them had actually accepted Yvonne's invitation to Thanksgiving dinner this year. Ryder had left the decision up to Clint, who hadn't taken more than three seconds to excitedly accept when Yvonne asked last night if they wanted to come.

Ryder tried to tell himself he was simply doing it because he knew Clint loved the Collins clan and the family gatherings. And it wasn't unusual for Yvonne and Leo to take Clint along with them to birthday parties and other celebrations. But he and Clint always did the bigger holidays—Thanksgiving and Christmas—alone.

Of course, he'd woken up this morning and was instantly sorry he'd let Clint make the call. Not because Ryder didn't want to go, but because his son had woken up with the flu, his fever reaching a hundred and two by early this afternoon. Clint had initially been devastated when Ryder told him they couldn't go to dinner, but that disappointment passed quickly enough to let Ryder know that the kid really did feel like shit.

He walked to the door, surprised to see Darcy there. "What are you doing here?"

"Happy Thanksgiving to you too." She lifted two plastic-wrapped plates. "I come bearing a feast."

"Yvonne promised to bring us some leftovers when they came home," he said, even as he stepped aside and she walked into the house, straight to the kitchen.

Ryder followed and watched as she put the plates on the counter. "Yeah...well...Leo, Lochlan, and Paddy looked pretty settled in with cigars and bourbon, and I figured it would be midnight before you saw any dinner. I snuck out before dessert, so I'm afraid there's no pie."

He was touched by her actions, but he also felt a bit guilty. "Darc, you didn't have to leave your family dinner. You live for those parties."

She gave him a look that screamed *seriously?* "Ryder, it's the social season. I'm going to party with all of them three more times before New Year's Day. Missing the last few hours of Thanksgiving isn't a big deal. Besides, I was determined to come over here to make sure you hadn't faked Clint's illness just to get out of having to say what you were thankful for."

He winked at her. "Dodged that bullet, didn't I? How long did it take to get through everyone?"

"Thirty-two minutes. I timed it."

"Jesus," he said, teasingly. "Aren't they going to wonder where you are?"

She hesitated for a moment. "Sunnie knows where I am."

"You told your sister you were coming here?" Ryder asked.

Darcy raised her hands. "I know we said we were going to keep our dating a secret, but I'd kind of already told my sister about that kiss in the elevator on Halloween, so when I said I was going to bring you guys some dinner..." She paused. "I have a very astute family. They notice everything."

Leo had warned him there was no such thing as a secret when with a Collins. And he didn't really mind if her sister knew. He'd really only suggested the secrecy to protect Clint. "It's okay, Buttercup. Is Sunnie the only one who knows?"

She shrugged. "Well, Pop Pop knows. And my mom and dad, which means Bubbles definitely knows too. And I think Paddy might suspect, and he'll probably tell Colm, who will say something to Kelli. Oh wait—Ollie winked at me as I was leaving the pub just now, so I have to assume that means he knows something too. But that's probably it. For now."

Ryder walked over and kissed her on the forehead, grinning. "Leo knows too."

"I didn't tell Leo, I swear."

He chuckled. "I did."

Her eyes widened. "You told Leo?"

"Why do you look so surprised?"

She considered his question for a second. "I didn't think you wanted anyone to know. I figured you'd be embar—"

Ryder narrowed his eyes, perfectly aware of where she was headed, and she stopped mid-word. "Were you going to say embarrassed? You thought I'd be embarrassed about us?" The words came out a little more hotly than he'd intended, but he didn't like that she'd thought that.

The way she didn't reply, didn't even move, told him that was exactly what she'd thought. "I know you think I'm too young. And...well...I *am* the babysitter. And you *are* my boss. And—"

"Darcy, I asked that we keep it a secret for Clint. That's it. If not for him, I wouldn't give a shit if the whole world knew you and I were dating."

Ryder wanted to suck the words back in the second they fell out...because Darcy's eyes lit up.

"Dating, huh?" she said, teasingly.

"Trial dating," he hastened to add, the damage already done.

She laughed and rolled her eyes but let his stupidly-justified semantics stand. "What about the people at work?"

He frowned. "You've told people there too?"

She shook her head quickly. "Oh my God. No. I didn't even tell my family. Sunnie was the one who connected all the dots when I was dipping out the plates for you and Clint." Then Darcy narrowed her eyes. "You know, it's sort of your fault too. You weren't exactly playing it cool at Friendsgiving. You were by my side the whole time, and then you said you were thankful for me and it was super sweet."

Ryder couldn't argue with her on that. He'd been unable to keep his hands to himself that night, sneaking his arm around the back of her chair at the dinner table, brushing his hand along her back when he thought no one was looking.

Even now, it was taking all the strength he had not to pull her in his arms and kiss her senseless.

"You're right. I wasn't playing it cool."

"I wouldn't tell anyone at work, Ryder. I swear. I know you're worried about that, and I would never jeopardize your career."

"All that shit I said about being your boss was bullshit. Workplace romances aren't against company policy. That was established when the president married his personal assistant a decade ago. Since then, two of the VPs have married other people within the organization." They were likely to catch some sideways glances if their relationship was revealed, but it wouldn't lead to either of them being fired. Past employment history had proven that.

"Oh. Well...good. And I explained to Sunnie about Clint, and she totally got it. No one in my family would ever—"

"I know they wouldn't, Darcy. It's okay. Honest."

"How is Clint?" she asked, her gaze landing on the can of chicken noodle soup he'd taken out to microwave for the kid.

"Fever broke a couple hours ago. Hasn't left bed all day, been complaining of a headache. He's actually slept more than he's been awake."

"That's what he needs, so that's good."

Ryder nodded. "He was really disappointed to miss Thanksgiving with your family."

"Yvonne told me. It's okay. It just means the two of you have to come to Christmas dinner now."

He rubbed his forehead and sighed, though the reaction

was more feigned than genuine. "What do you think my chances are of getting out of that?"

She giggled. "Slim to none."

He nodded and rolled his eyes. "Yeah. I figured."

"Bright side? You don't have to say what you're thankful for. And while yes, we do draw names, I can buy the gifts for whoever you and Clint get."

"I don't mind buying gifts."

"Really?"

"Really. And I'll let you tell Clint. It'll make him feel better about missing today. I was actually just going to make him soup. Not sure he's up to your leftovers feast tonight." He placed the second plate in the fridge as she grabbed the soup.

"I'll do that." Darcy turned and opened the can, pouring the contents into a bowl before adding the water and placing it in the microwave. Once the soup was heated, she took it out of the microwave, then put his plate of leftovers in. "You heat that up and eat and I'll take this back to the kiddo."

She reached into her large purse and pulled out a bottle of ginger ale. "Brought him this too in case his stomach was upset." She grabbed a glass, added ice, and poured.

Ryder tried not to focus on how much he loved watching her move around his kitchen like she lived there. "Thanks, Darc, but if you want to go back to the party—"

"Take a break and eat. Let Nurse Darcy take a shift." She picked up the bowl and glass and put them on a tray Yvonne had dubbed "the special tray," using it only to deliver breakfast in bed on birthdays. She left him alone in the kitchen with a huge plateful of some of the most delicious-looking food he'd ever seen. It beat the hell out of last year's Chinese food.

Once his meal was warm, he sat down in the kitchen and dug in gratefully. He'd planned to split the can of soup with Clint prior to Darcy's arrival, and he hadn't been looking forward to it. He rinsed his plate after he finished, then ventured down the hall to check on Darcy and Clint. He hovered just out of sight, outside the door, and listened to them talking.

"You sure you've had enough?" he heard Darcy ask. "I can make another can."

"No," Clint replied. "That was good. I was getting hungry."

Darcy laughed softly. "Then you're clearly getting better. Even so, what a shame to get sick on Thanksgiving. Couldn't even use the fever to get out of going to school for a day."

"I know. Right?" Clint clearly enjoyed her joke. "Think I can pretend I'm still sick long enough to miss on Monday?"

Ryder peered around the door, wanting to see them as well as hear. Neither of them noticed his presence. Clint was propped up on several pillows, Darcy sitting on the edge of his mattress.

"You? Stay in bed for three more days?" she asked. "I have my doubts."

Clint nodded earnestly. "Didn't think about that. Yeah. I need to get better by Saturday because me and Vince and a bunch of other guys are going to play touch football at Paulie's house."

"Sounds like fun." Darcy lifted the ginger ale from the

tray and placed it on his nightstand. "I'll leave that here for you. Do you need anything else? Want to watch TV? Play a video game?"

Eating appeared to have wiped out what little energy Clint had managed to muster. He shook his head. "No. I think I'm going to go back to sleep."

"Okay." Darcy placed her hand on his forehead, checking to see if his fever had returned. "Still cool as a cucumber."

Clint grinned at the familiar phrase. Ryder had heard Yvonne say it to both boys whenever they tried to feign an illness.

Then she helped him move a few pillows away and lie down again, pulling the covers over him.

"I'll check on you before I leave."

"I'll be asleep," he said.

Darcy shrugged. "That's okay. I'll just stand at the bedroom door and stare at you like a creepy stalker."

Clint laughed. "That's not what a stalker does."

She tilted her head as if he was off his rocker. "You sure?"

Clint nodded. "That's what moms do."

Ryder sucked in a deep breath, his chest suddenly tight as he watched Darcy bend forward to kiss his son on the forehead.

"Love you, kiddo," she whispered. "Feel better."

"Love you too, Darcy." Clint closed his eyes as Darcy quietly placed the empty soup bowl and spoon back on the tray.

Ryder slipped back into the hallway, leaning against the

wall, fighting against an onslaught of emotions he couldn't put names to.

When Darcy stepped out of the room, he straightened up and took the tray from her to place it on the floor.

"Hey," she said softly, "I thought—"

He shook his head as he pressed his fingers against her lips for just a second. Then he grasped her hand and led her to the end of the hallway to his bedroom. Dragging her inside, he closed and locked the door before pulling her body tightly against his and kissing her.

If Darcy was surprised by his impromptu actions, the feeling passed quickly as her hands circled his shoulders, touching the nape of his neck, holding him to her.

He'd done nothing but push her away since they'd started, so he understood her need to cling to him, to keep him close. Why should she expect that this time would be different? That he wouldn't keep shoving her away?

Together, they began to move backwards toward his bed. With each step, they continued to kiss, to shed clothing. He pulled his shirt off before hers, dropping them both to the floor. Darcy's hands were at his jeans, unbuttoning them, unzipping. She didn't even bother to push the denim over his hips, too impatient to touch what was beneath. Her hand wrapped around his cock at the same time he slid his fingers down the front of her pants and found her clit.

They hissed in unison.

"Clint," she whispered.

"We're going to be very quiet," he murmured. "But I... Jesus, I fucking need you, Darcy. Want you. Right now."

She smiled as she shoved her pants down, stepping out of

them and her panties. Her bra went next. Ryder matched her movements until both of them were naked. He wasted no time pulling her back to him, skin to skin, to kiss her once more.

They climbed onto the bed together. One of these goddamn times, he was going to take his time, draw it out, make it last all night.

This was not that time.

He bent his head lower, sucking her nipple into his mouth for just a moment before drifting lower to run his tongue along her slit. She was ready for him...always. It was a heady thing. To know that he could arouse this beautiful, intelligent, amazing woman with just his kisses.

"Can't wait anymore," she whispered.

Ryder crawled back up her body and placed his cock at her opening.

"I took my pill," she said softly.

He hadn't even thought, hadn't...

Ryder pressed inside her slowly, desperate to feel every single inch as he penetrated, filled. Claimed.

Darcy lifted her legs, wrapping them around his hips, drawing him in that last tiny bit. And then they moved together, slowly. Through it all, he kissed her, drinking in her lips and her quiet moans, certain he'd never tasted, never heard anything more wonderful.

It didn't take him long to reach the pinnacle. It never did with her. He reached down, stroking her clit, dragging her to the edge of the cliff as well. And when they dove in, it was together. His lips never left hers as they fell.

The entire encounter hadn't lasted more than ten

minutes, but as Ryder shifted to the side and pulled her to him, spooning her, he felt irrevocably changed.

Maybe he'd have regrets tomorrow, but tonight, he just felt thankful.

CHAPTER TWELVE

"Told you we were in trouble." Ryder grinned as they pulled into his driveway. Yvonne, with Reba in her arms, and Leo were there, waiting on the porch for him, Darcy, and the boys.

"We're late. I know," Ryder said, waving his hand in apology as they got out of the car. "Overtime. Sorry."

Clint and Vince were a lot less sorry. Probably because it had been one hell of a game, the Ravens winning after a Hail Mary pass that would probably be repeated on the Internet for the next decade as one of the greatest plays of all time.

Darcy was just as giddy. She and Clint had jumped up and down, screamed and hugged when the receiver caught the ball in the Ravens' end zone, winning the game and getting their team that much closer to a playoff berth.

While Ryder was thrilled as well, extending the season always meant a shit-ton more work for him.

"It's fine. We were watching the game on TV," Leo said.

"There was no way I would have left that game, either. Freaking awesome. That throw." Leo and Vince high-fived.

"I don't think your mom is going to be as understanding. She hates football," Yvonne said, walking to their minivan. "Vince, Clint, do you guys need anything from the house? Because if not, we have to hit the road now, or we're *all* going to be in the doghouse. You know Grandma Watson serves Sunday dinner at six thirty sharp."

Vince and Clint said they had everything they needed and, within five minutes, Yvonne had the baby in her car seat, the boys in the back, Leo behind the steering wheel, and all of them waving as they backed the minivan out of the driveway. He and Darcy waved from the porch.

"They're never going to make it on time," she said, her voice a bit hoarse from all the cheering.

"I know."

"So...you going to invite me in?" Darcy had met them here earlier, the four of them going to the football game together in one car.

Ryder's choice for a date had been box seats at the Ravens game with the boys. He'd wanted her to see that while, yes, he was a workaholic, there were some perks to putting in all those long hours. He also wanted her to see him with the boys. He knew *she* was great with them, but she hadn't had many opportunities to see him in dad mode for more than a few minutes at a time.

It had been the most fun he'd had at a game in years as the four of them ate their way through everything the snack bar offered and drank enough hot chocolate to float a yacht. It also helped that their team won.

Despite all that, Ryder realized he was standing at a

crossroads. He'd already let things with Darcy go way further than he'd intended. Her suggestions that they just go with the flow, test the waters as far as dating each other, had seemed good in theory because he'd expected the experiment to flop.

It hadn't.

And now when he combined the "official dates" with all the work and family events, happy hours, and lunch breaks, he realized they weren't trying anything on for size anymore.

They were dating.

He'd had ten long days since Thanksgiving to wrap his head around that. He wasn't sure he'd managed. And today was only going to muddy the waters more because he wasn't going to be smart, wasn't going to slow down the train.

Nope. Instead, he was testing one more thing, something dangerous that had the potential to seal his fate once and for all.

"I'm going to leave coming inside up to you," he said.

She grinned with delight. "Okay, then, I'm com—"

"Wait," Ryder said, turning to look at her. "If you come inside, Darcy, the kid gloves come off. You're still relatively inexperienced sexually, but the things I—"

"I'm coming in," she said.

He studied her face, read the determination there, and sighed. He wanted her so badly, he could taste it. Even if she'd said she wasn't ready to advance their play, he didn't doubt for a second, he still would have invited her in, cuddled with her on the couch, and given her all the missionary she could handle.

Maybe if he hadn't gone head to head with her since

Halloween and lost every single battle, he'd fight a little harder now. But the truth was, he loved losing to her.

He and Darcy had had sex three times, all of them far from his wildest encounters. Yet it was the best sex he'd ever had.

"As you wish," he said, dropping a line from *The Princess Bride* on her, loving the way it made her laugh.

He opened the door to his house and gestured for Darcy to enter before him.

Boomer was there, greeting them in true goofy, loving-dog fashion. The damn dog—*his* damn dog—barely spared him a glance as he jumped up on Darcy, his tail wagging a million miles a minute as the big mutt tried to tackle hug her. Darcy laughed as she bent down to pet him, giggling as Boomer licked her face. "Aw, I've missed you too, big guy."

"Boomer. Down," Ryder said. And because they'd done a shitty job training the dog and a great one spoiling him, it took Ryder three more times to get the dog away from Darcy.

Darcy turned toward him, laughing, but he shook his head, his expression stern as he pointed down the hallway. "My room."

He'd warned her what was coming, but Darcy—being Darcy—had viewed his words less as a threat and more as a challenge.

Unlike the dog, she took to his command like a fish in water, leading the way to his bedroom, her steps sure, even quick. They hadn't had sex since Thanksgiving. They'd both agreed what they'd done on the floor of his office couldn't happen again, professionalism too important to them, and with the Ravens certain to clench a playoff bid, his work hours would increase greatly, despite his desire to pull back as she'd suggested.

As for Darcy, she'd put in some long hours at work too then spent a great deal of time helping her family prepare for the Boob Voyage party for her godmother, Bubbles. The fact that they both lived in houses full of people didn't increase their chances for alone time, either.

Well, they had hours ahead of them now—and he intended to put them to good use.

Darcy still didn't understand how much he'd held back his own desires, determined to make her initiation into sex special and painless.

He couldn't offer her the same today. He wanted her with a need that overpowered every single voice in his head screaming that being with her was a mistake, something that would end in heartbreak.

As they entered his room, he closed and locked the door. No one else would be home for hours, but it was better to be safe than sorry. He didn't want Yvonne or Leo or—God forbid—the boys to return unexpectedly and catch them in the act.

She walked directly to the bed and ran her hand along his thick, soft duvet. Yvonne had helped him pick it out a few months ago after declaring his old one too threadbare to even be considered a quilt anymore.

"Take off your clothes," he demanded.

Darcy twisted toward him slowly, and he waited for her to either balk or perhaps give him that seductive smile of hers that tied his insides into knots.

She did neither. Instead, she pulled her Ravens jersey over her head and dropped it to the floor. The rest of her clothing fell away just as easily and without comment. Once she was completely naked, she faced him, chin held high, haughty as a queen.

She wasn't going to make this easy on herself. Or him.

Then he grinned. He liked a challenge too.

His wolfish expression finally triggered at least a smidge of self-preservation in her, as her eyes narrowed, but she didn't question him. She merely waited for his next command.

Ryder walked over to his closet and grabbed a handful of neckties. Joining her by the bed, he tossed all but one to the mattress.

"Turn around," he said.

Darcy complied, peering at him over her shoulder.

"Eyes forward," he barked.

She followed his directive, their eyes meeting briefly through their reflections when she discovered the mirror to his dresser was in front of her.

He stepped closer, his chest brushing her bare back. He reached for her hands and drew them behind her, securing them with his tie. Darcy tested the knot, but it held.

One of his favorite things about Darcy was the way she wore her hair down. The first couple of years of their acquaintance, ponytails and braids were the norm for her. Lately, she let it fall in long dark waves over her shoulders.

He swept the soft mass over one shoulder, capturing her eyes once more in the mirror.

"Watch me," he whispered as he pressed his lips to the side of her neck. Her head tilted to grant him better access. From his vantage point, he could see her tight nipples, begging for his fingers, his mouth.

Darcy must have noticed where his gaze had landed because, she thrust them forward the tiniest bit, a silent plea. He reached around her, taking a breast in each hand, squeezing the generous globes before pinching her nipples. Ryder listened to her slight gasp as he increased the pressure. His cock thickened when she groaned, the pinch of pain turning to pleasure.

She wasn't an inactive observer. With her wrists secured behind her back, he'd placed them in the perfect position for her to take matters—well, one matter—into her own hands. Darcy stroked his erection through his pants, and while he knew he should shift back or admonish her for it, he couldn't. Instead, he leaned into the pressure, loving the way she touched him.

Their play continued for several minutes, each of them taking their time to explore, to learn. Though hampered by his pants, Darcy still managed to drive him out of his mind with need. When she started to unfasten his belt, he knew it was time to regain control.

Ryder took a step away from her, placing his hand against the nape of her neck, using it to drive her forward. "Knees on the edge of the bed." He helped her kneel on the bed, continuing to push until her face was pressed against the mattress, her ass in the air.

"Stay like that," he said, when she tried to lower her rear end. Her stilted breathing was the only sound in the room. Despite the fact he'd put her in a vulnerable position, on display, she was obviously excited, ready. She wiggled her ass to entice him, and he worked hard to school his features.

Ryder stroked her ass, Darcy jerking slightly at the first caress. She'd clearly expected something harder.

He was in no hurry.

"Open your legs more."

She complied without hesitation. He had her exactly where he wanted her. Ryder ran his finger along her slit, from clit to anus. Darcy shuddered, gasped, then whispered, "More. Please."

"If you keep giving me orders, I'm going to gag you."

Darcy shuddered with arousal. "Okay," she whispered, and Ryder struggled to figure out if she was agreeing to his command or the gag.

"I don't want to do that. If I do anything that you don't like, say stop and I will."

She nodded. "I know that. I trust you."

Ryder was in over his head with her.

Trust was something he'd always struggled with, starting with his absent parents who'd let him down with every single missed baseball game and forgotten birthday. He'd learned at an early age the only person he could trust, could count on, was himself. He assumed that was why it was so difficult for him to form solid friendships. Why he struggled with commitment.

And Denise drove the lesson home when she'd cheated on him, left him.

"Darcy," he said, suddenly determined to call a halt, to get them out of this before it was too late.

"Don't hold back, Ryder. I know what you need. I need it too. Please."

Every time he thought he'd gained the upper hand, believed he'd gotten control of himself, she stripped him of it, until he felt as if he was standing before her completely bared—no walls, no secrets, no power to resist.

He swallowed heavily as he lifted his hand and brought it down roughly.

Darcy had jerked at his gentle touch, but now, as he spanked her, she actually sighed, groaned with pleasure, moved closer, tried to capture more.

Ryder spanked her a dozen times, her ass growing pinker with each blow. He pressed his fingers to her pussy, overwhelmed by how wet she was.

Darcy forcefully pushed back, trying to draw his fingers inside her. He pulled them away as she cursed.

"Dammit, Ryder!"

"Bad girl," he said with a grin as he peppered her ass with a half dozen more spanks.

"You have to fuck me. *Now!*"

He untied the knot around her wrists, dragging the silk away, and tossing it to the floor. Then in one quick motion, he flipped her to her back and climbed over her. He was still fully dressed, that fact lost on neither of them.

"I don't *have* to do anything."

She blinked several times. "Don't stop."

"I don't plan to. Unless you keep trying to take control. At which point, I will dress you, put you in your car, and send you home alone."

"You wouldn't dare."

He lowered his face to hers, kissing his way along her cheek until he reached her ear. "Try me," he whispered.

Darcy started to raise her hands—clearly worried about his threat, one he feared was definitely empty—intent on holding him.

He dragged her to the center of the bed, reaching for two more ties. He used them to bind her to his headboard before lowering his head and taking her nipple into his mouth with a suction he knew was painful. He repeated the action on her other nipple, letting himself imagine putting her in nipple clamps.

"God," she breathed. Her eyelids slowly drifted closed, almost dreamily. Darcy liked bondage. And pain. And being spanked.

He'd brought her here, determined to prove to his sweet little innocent that she was in over her head. Instead, he was the one getting schooled. Again.

Time to slow this down, to try one more time to grasp the reins.

Ryder rose from the bed, reaching over to open Darcy's legs even more. "Don't move. Don't speak."

Her body was flushed with arousal, the insides of her upper thighs slick, betraying how ready she was for him. He stood there, soaking her nakedness in. Memorizing every curve of her body. His gaze traveled the entire length of her, slowly, leisurely. Then he made the return trip.

She was completely naked, while he was fully dressed. He'd placed her in a vulnerable, submissive position, standing over her, asserting his authority, making sure she understood they were working on his timeline, with his game plan.

Her breasts rose and fell as she struggled to catch her breath. She licked her lips, then opened her mouth. He narrowed his eyes for a split second, warning her not to say anything, not even to plead, which was obviously her intent.

She closed her mouth, biting her lower lip in a way that was as endearing as it was seductive. Everything about

Darcy called to him. He wanted to mark her, claim her, make her swear that she'd always be his.

Only his.

But he knew that possession was a two-way street. He couldn't take her without offering himself.

Mine.

Yours.

He didn't allow himself to say either word.

Instead, he offered what he could. Darcy watched as he slowly stripped away his clothes.

"Did you take your pill this morning?"

She frowned as she nodded. "Yes," she whispered. "But if you—"

"No. Nothing between us. Ever."

Her legs parted even farther when he moved to join her on the bed.

Reaching into the nightstand drawer, he withdrew a tube of lubrication.

She gave him a shy, slightly embarrassed grin. "I don't think we need—"

"Shh," he admonished. "No talking unless it's too much and you need to say stop."

Darcy tilted her head curiously, and he knew she wanted to ask questions. He'd accused her once of asking too many. However, the wise woman held her tongue and waited patiently. The word *trust* floated through his brain again. She trusted him. And with every single action in his bed, she was proving it.

He lifted her legs, bending them until her ankles rested on the mattress near her ass, then he pushed her knees outward. Uncapping the lube, he squirted some on his finger.

When he pressed against her anus, her eyes widened, her mouth parted. He waited for her to tell him no, but she said nothing, just fought to suck in as much air as she could.

"Will you give me this virginity too?" he asked.

She licked her lips, taking her time to respond. He was glad. It meant she was thinking about it, not just giving him the answer he wanted to hear.

Finally, she nodded slowly.

"Not tonight," he said. "You're not ready."

A smile crept onto her face, and he realized what he'd done the moment he saw her genuine happiness. He'd just committed to another night with her. He didn't even pretend to be pissed off at himself. Another night with her was inevitable at this point. He couldn't fucking stay away.

"Tonight, we're just going to play." He pressed the tip of his finger in her tight ass, moving slowly, giving her time to adjust. "I'm going to buy you a butt plug," he murmured as he began to thrust his finger in and out, moving deeper with each return trip. "I'll bend you over my desk at work to slip it in, then send you back to your desk. You'll sit there, squirming, your ass filled with my toy, knowing that when I take it out, I'm going to replace it with my cock."

Darcy's breathing had grown louder with each word.

"Tomorrow," she whispered. "Do that tomorrow."

He chuckled. He'd teased her in his office about being a shitty sub, but that wasn't what he wanted from her at all. While he loved giving commands and having her obey, he also wanted her just like this, joking, fun, an equal partner.

Ryder's finger was completely lodged in her ass. The way she was lifting her hips, trying to draw it even deeper, told him she was all in on anal play.

Bending his head, he ran his tongue over her clit before sucking it into his mouth. Throughout, he continued to finger-fuck her ass. Darcy cried out, writhing beneath him, and he had to place a firm hand on her stomach to hold her still.

"God. Ohmigod," she gasped when he pressed his tongue inside her. Darcy came hard. And loudly. And he realized he was going to have to get a hotel room before they did this again.

He lifted his head as she started to come down from her orgasm, pulling his finger free.

He was used to her adorable, cat-who-ate-the-canary grins, so he was surprised when she hit him with the most seductive eyes he'd ever seen.

"Take me, Ryder. Hard."

He gritted his teeth, trying to find the strength to resist her, to call her to task for telling him what to do.

It was useless. He'd been a fool to believe he could ever control Darcy.

He lifted her legs, placing them over his shoulders, then he guided his cock to her and thrust inside with one swift, hard motion, burying himself to the hilt.

Darcy gasped and winced—fuck, he kept forgetting she was relatively new to this—but both reactions were fleeting. She tilted her hips so that he sank in even deeper.

"Hold on," he whispered.

And then he released the reins, gave in to all of his darkest desires. He took her hard and fast, pounding inside her even as she came again...and then again.

After her third orgasm, he withdrew, untied her hands,

and flipped her to her stomach, drawing her up on her hands and knees before driving back inside.

Darcy screamed. She was so tight and hot and wet.

And his.

She was fucking *his*.

His grip on her hips tightened when he realized her ass was still pink from his spanking. Though he didn't think it possible, his cock thickened even more. He spanked her as he thrust. Over and over.

Darcy arched her back, moved backwards to meet his inward thrusts.

Through it all, she begged for more. "God, Ryder. Yes! Fucking hell. Harder."

He gave her everything, unable to deny her.

As her fourth orgasm struck, he was there, spilling inside her, his climax so intense, it almost hurt.

Darcy's head dropped to the pillow beneath her as he remained in place, still kneeling, his cock going soft inside her.

He didn't move. He couldn't.

"Darcy," he whispered.

"Doggy style," she said, not bothering to lift her head from the pillow. "Big fan."

Ryder laughed, falling to the bed beside her. He was out of sex shape, muscles too long unused, twinging. "You're killing me, Buttercup."

"So what time should I be in your office tomorrow morning?"

He lifted his hand and brought it down on her ass hard, just once. And then, because he was a fucking fool, he said, "Eight o'clock, Ms. Young. Sharp."

CHAPTER THIRTEEN

"Ryder?" Darcy said, when he appeared in her mom's kitchen as she finished scooping out the melon balls. Sunnie, Yvonne, and Kelli had just finished putting the rest of the nip-petizers on the table and people were starting to show up for Bubbles's Boob Voyage party. "What are you doing here?"

He crossed the kitchen and gave her a sweet kiss on the cheek as he snuck a melon ball from the carved-out watermelon bowl. "You invited me."

"Yeah, but—"

"Never been invited to a party to say goodbye to a woman's boobs. Thought I should probably take advantage of the opportunity."

Darcy laughed. "A wise decision. Who knows when we'll get to throw another one of these?"

"If it was anyone other than you saying that, Buttercup, I'd agree. But I feel like the chances of this becoming something your family does...even for perfect strangers...seems high. Especially after looking at that table of food. The bowl of Mounds was a nice touch."

Darcy laughed. "That was my idea."

"Of course it was."

"What's that?" she asked, pointing to the gift bag in his hand.

"I brought Bubbles a present."

"Seriously? Who are you and what have you done with Ryder Hagen?" she teased. A week had passed since Ryder had taken her to his bedroom after the football game and opened her eyes to an entire world of—fuck-me-now— amazing sex.

While she'd begged him all week to follow through on his butt plug promise, Ryder insisted that they slow things down on the sex front. According to him, she was still too new to sex and he didn't want to rush her into anything she wasn't ready for.

Which was bullshit. Because she was ready for everything.

Every. Fucking. Thing.

Of course, it was hard to get pissed off at him for wanting to take his time and do things right because it convinced her that—while they still hadn't said those three little words— Ryder genuinely cared about her.

Neither of them referred to their dating as a trial run anymore. Instead, they appeared to just be going with the flow.

She'd been at work at eight on Monday morning, and they'd blown their "we're professionals" mantra out of the water, ruining their vow to eschew workplace hanky-panky. While he hadn't initiated her into anal sex, he'd convinced her that sixty-nine truly was the greatest number in the universe.

He'd gone to happy hour with her and Brooklyn on Wednesday, and afterwards they'd gone upstairs to her room for a quickie before he headed home to have dinner with his family.

Friday at work, he'd bent her over his desk on her lunch break to give her another taste of doggy style, which was indeed her favorite position thus far.

"I can assure you, it's me," Ryder said.

"Day drinking, then? Get an early start?" she asked.

Ryder laughed. "I'm completely sober." This time when he leaned in for a kiss, he skipped her cheek and went straight for her lips.

They parted at the sound of a wolf whistle from the doorway. "Don't stop on account of us," Bubbles said, entering the kitchen with Darcy's mom. "My girl parts are dusty, it's been so long. I'll have to live vicariously through you two."

"We wondered what was taking so long with the melon balls," Mom said. "So...is this Facebook-official yet?"

Darcy rolled her eyes. "Wow, Mom. That's not embarrassing at all."

"You're twenty-four, chica," Bubbles said. "Being embarrassed by your mom should be second nature to you by now."

Darcy didn't bother to disagree or point out that Bubbles was usually an active participant in anything and everything her mom did to embarrass her. It was a well-known fact to all of them. Not that Darcy would trade her mom or godmother for any other women on the planet.

"I suppose, um, congratulations are in order on your...

upcoming surgery," Ryder said, clearly out of his element. Just the fact that he'd shown up on his own made her so happy. And hopeful.

"Oh, bebe. It's long overdue. Look at these tits," Bubbles said, pointing at the girls. She'd really pulled out all the stops with today's party outfit, making sure the main attractions were spotlighted.

Ryder, whom Darcy had always thought fairly unshakable, actually flushed a little as his eyes drifted to Bubbles's shirt before he quickly looked away again, trying to be polite despite the open invitation.

"Very...um...impressive," he finally said.

Somehow Bubbles had managed to find an extremely lowcut sequined, zebra-print shirt that revealed no less than six inches of cleavage. Darcy figured chances were good they'd all get an eyeful of an escaped nipple at some point during the day, and there was no question in her mind every partygoer would be invited to "lift" one of Bubbles's tits to feel their weight.

"They're heavy as a dead donkey. Been carrying these girls around for too long. My back aches something awful these days," Bubbles explained.

"I've told her for years she should consider getting them reduced," Mom said.

"And as I told Riley," Bubbles continued, "these beauties were my moneymakers for a long time. Seemed disrespectful to just chop them off."

Ryder glanced at Darcy, confused. "Moneymakers?"

"Bubbles used to be a hooker in Vegas," Mom quickly explained. "And I'm not going to lie, it was her tits that first drew me to her. They're magnificent."

Darcy was fairly certain that was the exact moment Ryder regretted his decision to come to the party, but she was sure as hell glad he had, because she would remember—and laugh her ass off over—the dazed expression on his face for the rest of her life.

"Um," he said, but it was too late.

Mom and Bubbles were on a roll, both aware they had Ryder on the hook. Once they landed a fish, the Bubbles and Riley show was unstoppable. Darcy leaned forward, against the counter, to get a better view of Ryder's face.

"Offered Riley and Aaron a threesome for free, but you know Darcy's dad." Bubbles shook her head as if the decades-old memory was still a huge disappointment to her.

"It's that Boy Scout mentality of his," Mom said. "Never did manage to break him of that, did we, Bubbles? Though it wasn't for lack of trying."

Ryder looked at Darcy as if he expected her to be scandalized by the fact her godmother was a former hooker who tried to hook up with her parents.

"I've heard this story a million times," Darcy explained to him.

Ryder opened his mouth, but no sound came out. He needed to find his voice soon because, really, all his astonished silence was doing was giving Bubbles and Mom more time to play with him. They were like two cats toying with a mouse.

"Tell him about your doctor's appointment, Bubbles," Mom urged.

"Mom, I'm sure Ryder doesn't—"

Bubbles started as if Darcy hadn't said a word. "Well, I went to my regular doctor for a checkup. Make sure the hoo-ha and everything else was functioning okay. Hadn't gone in a couple years."

"Five years," Mom added. And she'd nagged Bubbles about that every single day of four of those.

Bubbles ignored the nag this time too. "Anyway, I'm sitting on the exam table, naked as the day I was born, with that paper gown over me."

"Paper gown?" Ryder asked.

"I'll explain later," Darcy murmured.

"And my doctor came in and asked if I had any concerns. I mentioned how I was thinking about a reduction. You know how doctors are."

Ryder shook his head.

Mom jumped in to respond. Primarily because she couldn't stand not being the storyteller. "She didn't give Bubbles a straight answer. Fifty percent one way, fifty percent the other. Gave her pros and cons and told her the decision was up to her. Hate when they don't just give you a straight answer. Anyway—"

Bubbles waved at Mom to hush. "Dammit, Riley. It's my story. Anyway...that conversation ends and the doctor tells me to lay down on the exam table for the titty squeeze."

Ryder looked at Darcy again.

"Breast exam," she amended.

"Jesus Christ," Ryder whispered as Darcy fought overtime not to laugh.

"So the doctor lifts the paper gown," Riley said.

"And there's this honest-to-God gasp," Bubbles said, grinning. "Don't you know that doctor looked me dead in the eye and said 'I one hundred percent support your decision to get the reduction.'"

"One hundred percent," Mom said gleefully.

"I looked at my doctor and said, 'You couldn't see what I had underneath that paper gown, could you?'" Bubbles continued.

"And the doctor said no," Mom added with a laugh, even though she hadn't even been in the damn exam room. "Of course, she would have known if Bubbles bothered to go see her regularly."

Bubbles was laughing as well. "So then the doctor says, 'God has been very generous with you.'"

"And Bubbles said, 'No, he hasn't,'" Mom finished.

Bubbles slapped Mom on the shoulder as they reached the punchline. "And then the doctor said, 'Well, there's an argument to be made for that as well.'"

Mom and Bubbles were laughing loudly at this point, and Ryder joined them, though Darcy wasn't sure if it was the amusing story or their reaction or maybe just horror over his current situation that drove it.

"What's going on in here?" Pop Pop said, walking in. "I hear laughing."

"Mom and Bubbles are telling Ryder the doctor story," Darcy said.

Pop Pop grinned, even as he shook his head. "Sorry to have missed it. That's a good one. Glad to see you here, Ryder," he added, shaking Ryder's hand. "We missed you and Clint at Thanksgiving. Darcy here says you took her to a Ravens game last week. Box seats."

Darcy rolled her eyes. Her grandfather had been very impressed by that tidbit.

Ryder smiled. "Perk of the job. Would love it if you joined us there for the next home game."

Pop Pop's eyes widened, and Darcy's heart skipped six full beats, knowing exactly how much that invitation would mean to her grandfather.

"I would like that very much indeed, son. Thank you so much. Well, how about that? Box seats. I need to go tell Paddy I won't be at the pub for the next game."

Pop Pop left quickly, and Darcy knew it wasn't just Padraig her grandfather was going to tell. She was pretty sure it wouldn't take him five minutes to tell the whole family he was going to be in box seats at a Ravens game.

"That was really nice of you," Darcy said.

"So," Bubbles said, eyeing the bag in Ryder's hand. "Did you bring Darcy a present?"

Ryder shook his head and held it out to Bubbles. "No. It's for you. I wasn't sure," he glanced back at Darcy, "if this was one of those occasions that called for a gift."

Bubbles's eyes lit up as he handed her the festive gift bag. "Damn, chica. This one is a keeper." Even though there was an entire table of presents out in the dining room, Bubbles tossed the tissue paper out and reached into the bag, laughing loudly as she pulled out what looked like a coloring book and a pack of colored pencils.

Mom peered over Bubbles's shoulder as she began flipping through the pages and started laughing as well. "I dibs the one that says, 'We never talk anymore. I like that.'"

"Let me see." Darcy grabbed the coloring book—and cracked up. Every coloring page contained an insult. "Oh my God. It's perfect!"

Ryder shrugged. "Yvonne said you'd be laid up for a couple of days after your surgery. Thought that might help you pass the time."

Darcy was speechless as Bubbles and then her mom hugged Ryder, proclaiming it a wonderful gift, before they walked out of the kitchen to rejoin the party.

Ryder glanced her direction and frowned. "What? What's wrong?"

"I..."

Darcy stopped short, overthinking the fuck out of everything. It had been on the tip of her tongue to tell him she loved him, but...what if the timing was wrong? What if it was too soon? What if it pushed him away? She didn't want to screw up one second of this day because everything was so damn perfect.

"I'm glad you came," she said instead, too loudly, too stupidly.

He laughed. "I thought it sounded like fun, but now I'm not so fucking sure. What the hell did she mean by paper gown? And you knew your godmother was a hooker in Vegas?"

"She wanted to be a stripper," Darcy said, as if that made a single bit of difference.

"Ooookay."

"But she can't dance. Now the joke is maybe she was just too top-heavy all along and after the reduction, she'll become a Rockette."

"Darcy," he said.

"Yeah?"

"Your family is insane."

"Tell me about it," she joked. "You know...for someone who says they don't like crowds Bund noise, you seem to keep putting yourself in the thick of it with my family."

"Not sure why they seem to be the exception. There

wasn't a lot of laughter in my house when I was growing up, so I guess I told myself I preferred things that way. I was obviously wrong." He paused for a moment, his face suddenly serious. "Your Pop Pop called me 'son'."

Darcy didn't know how to reply to that. Didn't even know how to *think* about that. Ryder had mentioned that his family wasn't close, but he hadn't gone into great detail or told her why. "Is that okay?" she asked.

Ryder nodded, and Darcy tried to read his expression. It looked like he was...touched. And his smile returned tenfold. "Yeah. Yeah, it is."

"I think you might have just made his year with that invitation to the football game."

Ryder's grin faltered a bit. "I'm sorry I never issued it before. I knew he was a big Ravens fan. Not sure why I didn't think of it."

She gave him a kiss on the cheek. "It was very sweet of you."

Ryder reached for her before she could pull away and gave her a much longer and less sweet kiss. There were times —like now—when Ryder kissed her with so much passion, she struggled to breathe.

"Damn. Get a room."

Ryder and Darcy parted as Oliver peeked his head in.

"Sunnie told me to come get you two. We're about to start playing Pin the B-Cup on Bubbles."

"We're on our way," Darcy said as Ryder shook his head and chuckled.

"How long do we have to stay before I can steal you away to your place? Bubbles wasn't the only one I bought a present for."

"I'm supposed to stay and help clean up afterwards, dammit. Hang on." She closed her eyes, thinking hard.

"What are you doing?

"Trying to remember if I have any blackmail on Sunnie or Finn that I can use to get out of it."

Ryder wrapped his arm around her shoulder. "I'll help you clean up. That'll make it go faster. Then it's you and me all night."

"All night?"

He nodded. "Cleared it with Leo before I headed over here."

Darcy didn't even bother to hide her delight.

Best. Day. Ever.

CHAPTER FOURTEEN

Darcy giggled as Ryder hastily pushed her into her bedroom, tossed his overnight bag down, then closed and locked the door behind them.

"Don't get me wrong. It was a great party, but I never thought we'd get here," he said as he pulled her shirt over her head, his quick actions to divest her of her clothing, backing up his words.

"Me, either."

It appeared she was anxious to get him undressed as well, considering they were both naked within seconds. Their time alone was precious little, so when they managed to get somewhere private, clothing was typically the first thing to go.

Kissing Darcy was seriously becoming his favorite thing to do, and he found himself attempting to steal those kisses from her as often as he could. He ran his hands through her hair, his lips traveling along her soft cheek to her neck, to that little spot that never failed to provoke the cutest squeak.

He grinned when he hit the jackpot. Then he nipped her earlobe and she giggled.

"All good on birth control?" he whispered.

She nodded, and he started to kiss her again, surprised when she pulled away. "Why do you always ask me that?"

Ryder blew out a quiet sigh as he pondered what to say. In truth, he wasn't sure why she hadn't asked him that question before.

And on the flipside, he was pissed at himself for continuing to succumb to these stupid doubts that wouldn't leave him alone. "I'm sorry, Darcy. I shouldn't do that. But..."

"But?" she prompted.

He ran his hand through his hair, suddenly uncomfortable. He and Darcy had been together several times now, and more often than not, a memory of Denise found a way to sneak into the bedroom with him and fuck him up.

He considered shrugging off her question, attempting to distract her from her curiosity with more kisses. Finally, as always, he gave her the truth. "Denise was pregnant when we got married. That's *why* we got married. We'd only been dating a few months. One night I didn't have a condom. She said she was on the pill and..."

"She wasn't on the pill?"

Ryder shrugged. "I don't know the answer to that. When she found out she was pregnant, she said she'd forgotten to take it a few days, that she thought it would be okay."

"Alright. I get that. But if you're worried, then why not use a condom with me?"

Ryder studied her face for a long time. "The truth is, Darcy, I..."

It was on the tip of his tongue to tell her that he trusted her.

That he loved her.

Fuck.

He felt a little bit light-headed as he looked at her and realized...

This had all gone way too far.

He swallowed deeply, trying to push his stomach, which was now lodged in his throat, back down.

What the fuck had he done?

"It's okay. Forget I asked," she whispered, taking in what he was sure must have been one hell of a deer-in-the-headlights look on his face.

She was letting him off the hook because Darcy knew him too well, saw things he didn't intend for her to see.

She gave him a sweet—God, *hopeful*—smile, and his guts twisted. The woman didn't have an ounce of self-preservation, insisting on looking at him like some goddamn Prince Charming or Westley or...

Panic mingled with anger and confusion and frustration.

Not a good combination.

He'd *told* her he didn't want this. But she didn't listen to him, didn't heed his warnings.

She stepped closer to him and placed a hand on his cheek. "Don't ask me about the birth control again," she said softly. "If it's not safe, I'll tell you. I promise."

Ryder remained motionless for a second or two, uncertain where to go from here. Part of him was telling him to take the high road, to be a smart man, put his clothes back on and get the hell out of there.

That wasn't the part that was going to win.

Unfortunately, neither was Prince Charming. Darcy wasn't getting roses and candlelight and soft words tonight.

"Get on the bed. Hands and knees."

She did exactly as he said, even going so far as to taunt him by wiggling her ass.

He sucked in a deep breath and fought for control. Right now, he was walking a razor's edge, but he seemed incapable of turning back.

He went to his bag to grab the present he'd told her about earlier.

She grinned at him over her shoulder.

"Eyes forward." The words came out harsher, louder than he'd intended. If that frightened her, she gave no indication, merely turned to look away once more.

He approached the bed and sat next to her, running his hand over her bare ass, stroking it just once before smacking it a few times. Hard.

Darcy sighed and arched her back. "Please, Ryder."

He rubbed the back of his neck, his heart racing at her plea.

He tossed a tube of lubrication and the butt plug he'd bought her on the bed next to her so she could see them.

"That's where we're going tonight." His words sounded threatening to him, but damn if Darcy failed to pick up on it.

"Yes," she whispered.

Wrong answer.

She was giving him the wrong answers.

He was overwhelmed by the need to protect her, to give her the man she deserved, but he'd never lied to her. Not once. And he couldn't start tonight.

He spanked her again, over and over, not stopping until

her ass and upper thighs were a deep pink. Darcy cried out a few times, but she never asked him to stop.

No. Instead, she lowered her head to the mattress, her ass still high, offering him perfect submission.

"Your safe word is 'elevator.' Say that, and it all stops. Say anything else and I keep going. 'No' won't work tonight. Neither will 'stop.'"

She shuddered as she turned her head to look at him. Her flushed face revealed her arousal. "Okay."

"Say it now," he demanded.

"Elevator."

He nodded, then climbed on the bed, kneeling behind her. Bending over her, he gripped her hands and pulled them to the wrought iron headboard. "Hold on to the bars. Don't let go. If you think you can't manage that, I'll find something in your closet to tie you up."

"I can hold on," she reassured him. "I won't let go. Promise."

He knew how much she loved being tied up, so he didn't mistake her promise as reticence.

Unfortunately.

No. Darcy truly wanted to submit.

They'd been inching toward this for weeks, merely dipping their toes in, as he gave her a taste. She'd confessed yesterday in his office that her cousin, Caitlyn, had married a dominant man, BDSM a big part of their sex lives. The two of them had been eating lunch together, sitting together on his couch, talking.

She was so damn easy to talk to.

Last night, Ryder had tossed and turned for hours as he played out scene after scene of he and Darcy together. Sex swings, spanking benches, nipple clamps, ball gags. In his mind, he'd placed her in all of it, and he'd jerked himself to completion three times before he'd managed to finally fall asleep.

When he'd woken up this morning, all he could think about was seeing her. So he'd accepted Yvonne's last-ditch-attempt invitation to the Boob Voyage party, stopping at a bookstore for Bubbles's gift and a sex shop for Darcy's.

He'd pulled Leo aside at the party to ask if he and Yvonne were okay with all three kids on their own tonight. Leo had grinned, said of course, then given him that worn-out dad advice, "if you're gonna tap it, wrap it," chuckling as he did so.

Ryder picked up the lubrication as Darcy held the position he'd put her in. Her grip on the headboard tightened when he stroked her slit. She was soaking wet and turned on, excited.

Darcy was adventurous, an enthusiastic partner. While still relatively innocent, she knew exactly what she wanted in bed.

Another curse—or blessing—of her being a part of a large family with lots of older cousins and her sister, Sunnie. The Collins women didn't appear to hold back when it came to sharing confidences or answering Darcy's questions. As such, it had allowed her to form her own opinions and contemplate her own sexual desires, so that when she came to his bed, she'd had an entire list of things she genuinely wanted to experience.

No restraint. No fear.

He squirted some lube on his finger, rubbing it around her anus.

Darcy breathed out loudly, excitedly. "God, Ryder. I love this all so much."

Ryder grinned. Smugly. He couldn't help it. He felt the same way.

He slowly pressed his index finger inside her, to the first knuckle, then the second.

"Breathe," he murmured when he realized she was holding her breath. She blew out a long stream of air, shuddering as she did so.

He pushed that one finger in and out for a couple of minutes, giving her time to adjust. He'd bought her a small butt plug, the toy probably not bigger than two of his fingers. He didn't want to scare or hurt her, recalling Denise yelling at him the night he'd tried this with her, telling him he was too rough, it was too painful, that he always pushed her too far.

He hoped that by initiating Darcy slowly, gently, it would increase the odds that she'd want to try it again, would eventually let him take her ass, to live out so many of those fantasies he'd played out in his mind.

Ryder shook that thought loose. Let it drift away. At some point, he was going to have to find the strength to walk away.

So he'd give her this—her first taste of anal play—and leave her future forays to...

Fuck.

He let that thought fly away too. The image of Darcy with another man went through him like knives, and for a moment, he was actually jealous.

Jealous of future lovers Darcy might take to bed?

It was preposterous.

Ryder had never been jealous a day in his life, not the type to ever work up that kind of passionate response. Hell, he hadn't even sought retribution against the other man in Denise's life because, in the end, he hadn't been able to summon up enough emotion to care.

He dismissed all of that, hating the way his thoughts were all over the place. He needed to concentrate on the task at hand. He was too distracted, too in his own head.

Adding more lube to his fingers, he pressed in once more, this time with two.

Darcy gasped, but she didn't release the headboard, nor did she try to pull away. "That feels…"

He slowly started thrusting, Darcy moving in tandem, not merely accepting the penetration but enjoying it.

"Damn," she breathed. "Love…love this."

Ryder stretched her for a couple minutes more before withdrawing and picking up the butt plug. "This is a little bit thicker but not by much. You okay to try it?" he asked, shocking himself with the question. With past lovers, he simply took charge, did what he wanted, and trusted the women in his bed would use their safe words.

Darcy was too young, too new to this. Safe word be damned. They were going to talk this out together.

"So okay," she said with a soft laugh.

He squeezed lube onto the toy, then pressed the tip against her ass. "Don't forget to breathe," he murmured as he slowly pushed it in.

Darcy sighed and groaned, telling him without words how much she loved what they were doing. Once it was fully lodged, he lowered his head and bit her cute little ass.

Darcy jerked and laughed but never loosened her grip on the headboard.

"Roll over." Ryder wanted to see her face. While she was a big fan of doggy style, he preferred to watch her face when she came.

Darcy flipped over, but damn if she didn't keep her hands above her head, resuming her hold on the bars.

Ryder lowered himself until his chest was pressed to hers. They kissed as he rubbed her clit, bringing her to the brink of a climax, again and again, backing away at the last second each time.

Darcy was breathing heavily, flushed, and cursing a blue streak.

"Oh my God. Don't stop!" she yelled at him. "I swear to fucking God, if you—"

He kissed her roughly, nipping her lower lip. "Who's in charge here, Darcy?"

She narrowed her eyes, her need for release too strong. "Dammit! Ryder—"

"Who?" he repeated, his gaze locked on hers. "Tell me who."

She hesitated just a moment before whispering, "You."

"Who do you belong to?"

Ryder didn't have a clue where that question had come from, but he wasn't leaving this bed without the right answer.

"You. Always."

Her response was instant—and it sent a piercing pain through his chest even as he savored every damn syllable.

"That's right. You do. Don't forget it."

He gripped his cock, lined it up, and thrust to the hilt, her pussy even tighter with the plug in her ass.

Her back arched as she came instantly.

Ryder didn't give way to her orgasm. He couldn't. He thrust rapidly with all the strength he had. Over and over, he pounded into her body, taking everything she had to offer, unable to hold back a single thing. He wanted to give it all to her. All of him.

Her first orgasm gave way to a second, and he still rocked inside her, harder and harder. Darcy's fingernails scored his back, the sting only driving him higher.

"Fuck, Darcy," he groaned as his balls constricted. He was lost. Lost inside her, and he never, ever wanted to be found.

"Oh, oh, oh!" she panted, her third orgasm triggering his.

He clenched his eyes tightly as pleasure and pain mingled, became the same damn thing.

Ryder held himself over her for a full minute after his climax had passed, refusing to open his eyes, knowing he'd give too much away.

When he felt as if he could control his expression, he looked at her.

"You okay?" he asked, suddenly aware of just how roughly he'd taken her.

She nodded. "That was amazing. I think I'm starting to understand how people can become sex addicts."

He chuckled, withdrawing and dropping next to her. Leave it to Darcy to find a way to make him laugh, even when he felt so raw inside.

Ryder slowly drew the plug out of her ass as she shuddered, still trying to come down from her orgasms.

He dropped the plug to the floor. He'd deal with that later. Right now, he was boneless, physically exhausted.

Darcy kissed his jaw sweetly.

"I want to take you out to dinner tomorrow night," he said.

She lifted her head and smiled at him like he'd invited her to fly to Paris with him. "Okay. You still staying the night tonight?" she asked tentatively, clueing him in to the fact that he had a bad habit of pulling away after sex.

"Unless you want me to leave."

"Hell no." She wrapped herself around him, her arm around his waist, his chest serving as her pillow.

He closed his eyes, soaking up how good it felt to hold her in his arms like this. He lay there for a long time, relaxed, at peace, as Darcy slept.

He was just about to fall asleep himself when he heard her whisper, "I love you."

Ryder didn't move, didn't respond. Hell, he wasn't sure he was even breathing.

She'd obviously waited until she'd thought he was sleeping to say those three words.

Sleep deserted him.

She loved him.

And he loved her.

What the fuck was he supposed to do now?

CHAPTER FIFTEEN

"Hey, Darc. Over here."

Darcy glanced across the pub and saw Oliver waving to her.

"Come meet some buddies of mine from work," he said as she approached. She and Ryder were meeting here for a drink and then going to dinner later.

As far as she was concerned, their trial run had been over for weeks, and she planned to tell him that tonight. She wanted to say she was his girlfriend, and she wanted to scream it to the world.

Equal parts anxious and excited, she'd gotten ready early and decided to wait for him in the pub instead of upstairs.

Gavin wolf-whistled at her. "Somebody must have a hot date. You look awesome, Darcy."

She hip-checked him appreciatively. "Thanks."

She'd known Gavin nearly a decade, the man as much a cousin to her as her real cousins. Her uncles Sean and Chad and her aunt Lauren had taken in quite a few foster kids over the years, some remaining weeks, others months. Gavin had moved in when he was fifteen and stayed.

"So what are you guys up to?" she asked.

"We finished a big project today and we felt like celebrating," Oliver explained. He and Gavin did construction for Uncle Killian and Uncle Justin, as well as Oliver's dad, Sean. Darcy suspected that one day it would be Oliver and Gavin taking over the reins of J and K Construction when all of her uncles were ready to retire. "Let me introduce you." Oliver pointed to the other three men standing at the bar with him. "This is Roger. And Deke. And that big guy next to you is Ron."

Darcy shook hands with Roger and Deke, turning to smile at Ron. "Nice to meet you."

"You too," Ron said. "Ollie says you're an artist or something?"

"Graphic art," she explained. "I let a computer do all the hard work for me. If I had to feed myself with my paintings or sketches, I'd starve."

"Hey, don't sell yourself short. I'm shit with computers," Ron said affably. "I swear to God, machines hate me. I've gotten to the point where I just get my eleven-year-old to handle all the computer stuff."

"Oh, kids are always the most tech-savvy ones in the room."

"My daughter teases me about it all the time, but without her, I'd probably still be trying to figure out how to join Myspace."

Darcy laughed. "Sounds like you've got a gr—"

Darcy broke off mid-sentence when two hands appeared

in her peripheral vision, fists gripping Ron's shirt and pulling him away from her.

She twisted just in time to see Ryder throw the mother of all punches, knocking Ron to the floor.

"What the f—" she started, but Ryder wasn't looking at her, his focus solely on Ron.

"Stay the fuck away from her!" Ryder said hotly, bending over, ready to continue the fight. Oliver and Gavin rushed him, each taking an arm and pulling him away from Ron, who remained on the floor, his hands out in obvious surrender.

"Jesus, Ryder," Oliver said. "Chill out, man. They were just talking."

If Ryder heard Oliver, he gave no indication. He was still furious, staring Ron down, hard. "Stay away from her."

"What's going on here?"

Darcy turned to see her dad coming from the adjoining restaurant, Sunday's Side. Padraig had already come around the counter to step between the men and to help Ron up.

"You okay, man?" Padraig asked Ron, who simply nodded, his gaze never leaving Ryder's, which seemed smart.

Ryder was far from cooling off. Completely out of control. His face blood-red, his eyes dark with rage, his expression murderous, as he struggled to break free from Oliver and Gavin's grip. It was definitely taking both men—who were strong as oxen—to hold him back.

Darcy felt like she was looking at a stranger.

"Ryder. Please," Darcy said, flabbergasted by his jealousy, searching for a way to calm him down. It was a fruitless attempt, as he never glanced her direction.

Dad stepped between the two men, looking as confused as she felt. "Ryder, son. You need to calm down. Now."

Her dad spoke with a quiet authority. He was also wearing his police uniform, his badge, and his gun belt. It was his night to work. He always stopped by before clocking in to grab a quick dinner with Mom.

Ryder was breathing rapidly, his chest rising and falling. And while he wasn't struggling to break Oliver and Gavin's grip anymore, neither man was letting him go, either. Probably because Ryder genuinely looked like one word would flip the switch again and he'd go back in for blood.

Dad turned toward Ron, taking in the bright red, swollen spot high up on his cheek from Ryder's punch. He was going to have a black eye tomorrow, no doubt about it. "You okay?"

Unlike Ryder, Ron was calm, almost subdued. "Yeah."

"Dad..." Darcy started, though she didn't have a clue what to say. She didn't understand a damn thing that was going on at the moment.

Dad gave her a regretful look, then looked back at Ron. "You want to press charges?"

Ron shook his head quickly, his eyes darting over to Ryder with something like...

Regret?

Darcy wondered if they knew each other.

"No. I'm good." Then Ron turned to the other guys he'd been drinking with. "I think I'm gonna take off. See y'all next week at work."

No one replied, not a single word, as Ron left the pub. It wasn't easy to render her or her family speechless, but with one punch, Ryder had managed.

Dad turned back toward Ryder, but before he could say anything, Oliver was releasing his hold on Ryder's arm.

"What the fuck, man? What's wrong with you? Ron's a good guy."

Ryder snorted angrily. "A good guy..." he murmured.

Whatever white-hot rage had been coursing through Ryder started to evaporate, and for the first time since entering the pub, he looked at Darcy.

"Ryder?" she said softly, searching his face for some sort of sign of why he'd snapped so unexpectedly.

His voice when he spoke was wooden, his face completely closed to her. "I told you I couldn't do this, Darcy. Told you from the beginning."

His words went through her like daggers because there was no mistaking where this was going. And Darcy didn't have a clue how to stop it.

"Ryder, wait," she said, holding her hands up, trying to step closer.

He shook his head. "No. I don't want this. I don't want *any* of this. I can't do it again. Any of it. I told you that, but you didn't listen."

He kept repeating himself, working hard to drive his point home.

"Let's just take a minute. Maybe we can go—"

"This is over."

"Please," she whispered. "You have to help me understand why—"

"I have to go."

He turned without saying goodbye, and she started to follow. Ryder must have seen her move, read her intent to chase him, because he spun back around.

"Don't," he said hotly.

She blinked rapidly, fighting the tears threatening to fall.

"Don't follow me." He must have seen her distress because his eyes softened for just a moment. "This is for the best, Darcy. You have to believe me when I say that."

"No." She shook her head, but his mask fell back into place. "Please. Don't do this. I lo—"

"Stop." Ryder shut her down quickly, wincing as if she'd struck him. "I'm sorry," he whispered, as he turned once more and headed toward the door.

Darcy took one step to follow before her dad gently grasped her hand to stop her.

"I think you should let him go for now, Darcy."

She paused. If her dad hadn't added the words *for now*, she would have shrugged off his grip and run after Ryder no matter what anyone said.

"I don't understand what happened."

Dad gave her a sympathetic smile, then gestured toward an empty booth near the back of the pub. "Why don't we have a seat over there? We can talk."

She went with him, the two of them sitting across from each other. Padraig followed them over, clearly concerned. "You okay, Darc?"

She nodded once, then shrugged. "I'm confused and..." She shook her head. "No. I'm not okay."

"I'm sorry, sweet pea." Padraig placed a soft kiss on top of her head. "You need anything right now?"

Darcy shook her head again, struggling to speak—her throat was closing up.

"Aaron?"

Dad said, "No thanks, Paddy. I'm on duty later."

"Okay. Wave me down if you change your mind." Padraig left them alone.

Dad reached across the table to grasp one of her hands in his. "Maybe we should take this from the top. It seemed pretty obvious at Bubbles's party that you and Ryder are seeing each other."

"Yeah. We've been going out."

"When did that start?"

"Halloween. We were both trapped in the elevator during the power outage for a few hours."

Her dad's eyebrows rose. "And this is the first I'm hearing of that? Why wouldn't you have called me to get you out?"

Darcy grinned. Her dad would always be overprotective. She held her other hand out. "It was a city-wide power outage on Halloween. I'm sure you were needed elsewhere."

"Yeah. Okay. So Ryder..."

"Ryder," she said sadly.

"He's older than you are," Dad said.

"I know."

"And your boss."

Darcy grimaced. "You're not saying anything Ryder hasn't said himself."

"Neither one of those things is a problem?"

"No," she said. "They aren't."

Dad considered that, rubbing his jaw. "His wife has been gone...what...three, four years?"

"Four."

"Still grieving?" he asked.

"I didn't think so. I...don't know." As Dad's interrogation continued, she realized the cop in him was trying to gather all the evidence in hopes of understanding why Ryder Hagen, the least emotional man she'd ever known, had just flipped his fucking lid because she was talking to a stranger.

"How serious are things between the two of you?" Dad asked.

In Darcy's mind, they were as serious as they got. She'd fallen head over heels for him years ago. And she'd just begun to think those feelings were reciprocated. She knew Rome wasn't built in a day, but dammit, she'd really believed construction was well underway. Until tonight.

"Ryder's been resistant to dating anyone again. Says he likes his unencumbered, workaholic life. Plus, there's Clint to think of."

"And you changed his mind about that?"

She casually lifted one shoulder. "I suggested a trial run."

"How many dates have you had?"

Darcy closed her eyes wearily. "Probably like a dozen."

Dad chuckled. "Doesn't sound like a trial to me. Sounds like you're dating."

"We are. It was real—all of it. At least...to me."

Her father sobered up. "You're in love with him."

Darcy didn't hesitate to respond. She nodded, swallowing heavily, fighting overtime not to cry.

"When Ryder said he couldn't do this, what did he mean?"

"His marriage to Denise..." Darcy tried to figure out how she could explain without sharing more than she should. She longed to open up and pour her heart out to her dad, but so much of this wasn't her story to tell. "There were some problems. It's affected the way he sees himself. He blames himself, says he wasn't a good husband. Plus, I think, since her death, he's struggled with trusting other people. He's closed himself off to the idea of falling in love again because he had his heart broken. So now he's told himself he's not capable of being in a relationship."

Dad leaned back and blew out a long, slow breath. "Trust in a relationship—"

"Is everything. I know that, Dad."

"Jealousy is—"

"A horrible thing," she interjected.

Dad chuckled. "You're just like your mom. She never gives me a chance to get a word in edgewise, either. What I wanted to say is, trust in a relationship takes times to develop, and jealousy is often the fallout until that trust is built."

"He punched a guy, Dad. I hadn't said more than three sentences to Ron. I wasn't flirting, I swear."

"I didn't say you were. When it's the beginning of a relationship and a man reaches that point where he's in love, but still in denial, jealousy isn't all that uncommon."

"You've never been jealous with Mom."

Dad laughed. "You're joking, right? Vegas?"

Darcy frowned. "What about it? You and Mom ran off to Vegas and eloped. It was super romantic."

"Wow. It appears your mom and I must have left big chunks out of our marriage story. We weren't dating when we went to Vegas, and we didn't go there together to elope. I followed her there, in a jealous rage because she'd flown across the country with a married man."

"Wait. What? Who?"

"Trevor Blankenship."

"The guy who ran off with the stripper and got lost in the desert? The one who was your best man? I thought he went to Vegas with you *and* Mom."

Dad shook his head, chuckling. "Good God, no. Trevor had gotten in a fight with his wife and they'd separated. He and Riley were both in a funk, and drunk, and your mother got it in her head the two of them should take a trip to Vegas to cheer themselves up."

"Sounds like her," Darcy said. "I mean the trip part, not the married-guy part."

"Because that part wasn't true. And if I'd been thinking clearly, thinking like a man who wasn't wearing his heart on his sleeve, I probably would have had a less stressful eight-hour cross-country journey to Sin City. Instead, I'd worked myself up into a jealous lather. One that dissipated the second I saw your mom at the blackjack tables, laughing and having the time of her life."

"Where was Trevor?"

"Draped around the stripper."

Darcy laughed. "I can't believe I've never heard that part of the story. I mean, I knew about the jealous estranged wife showing up, and the stripper and Trevor getting in trouble with the mob or something, and Bubbles helping you look for them, but I didn't realize you hadn't all traveled together."

"I've never said this to Riley, so if you repeat it to her, I'll flat-out deny it, but her running off to Vegas with Trevor was the best thing she's ever done. It forced me to pull my head out of my ass and see what was standing right in front of me."

Darcy wiped away a tear, loving her father's story, even as her own heart was breaking. "Pop Pop said the same thing happened with him and Grandma Sunday. He thought she could do better, so he pushed her away. But I don't see how that's the same as what just happened here."

Dad reached for her hand again. "That's because you're too close to it. You said Ryder wasn't happy in his marriage, that he struggles with trust and love. You think that's impacting his feelings for you?"

"Yeah. I do."

"Well, I have a different perspective because I was standing in the opening between the pub and restaurant when Ryder walked in. I saw his face when he spotted you with that Ron guy." Dad took a deep breath and, because she knew her dad, she understood that he was trying to find the right words.

With her mom, whatever popped into her head came out. But Dad was different. He always carefully considered what he wanted to say. Which was probably why she and her mom could have knockdown, drag-out arguments whenever they disagreed, but with her dad...just a few gentle, well-chosen words from him on something he thought she was doing wrong would have her thinking for days.

"What did you see?" she asked.

"A man doesn't throw a punch over a woman he doesn't care about."

Darcy let that sink in deep, took the words as the gift they were. Unfortunately, they didn't change what had just happened. Ryder wasn't finished fighting this thing between them. What if he never did?

"What do I do, Dad? How do I fix this?"

Dad smiled sadly. "That's the problem. You don't. Ryder does."

"But—"

"I'm going to say a word, and you're not going to like it."

Darcy closed her eyes because she knew what was coming.

"Patience. You're going to have to let Ryder figure this out and come to *you*. If you keep pushing, Darcy..."

"I'll push him away."

CHAPTER SIXTEEN

Ryder opened the front door just as Padraig reached the top step. He'd heard the car pull in the driveway. He'd expected it to be Darcy, so he was surprised when he saw her cousin climbing out of the vehicle.

"Let me guess. I'm banned from the pub," Ryder said, still struggling to believe last night was real. It had felt a little bit like an out-of-body experience. He could see himself storming across the bar, throwing the punch, losing his shit, breaking Darcy's heart, but he couldn't quite connect the dots, make that man fit with the man he was today...who just felt numb.

"You're not banned. I was hoping maybe we could talk for a few minutes."

"Did Darcy send you here?"

Padraig rolled his eyes. "Gonna let you answer that yourself because it'll tell me how well you know my cousin."

Ryder shook his head. "No. She didn't. Darcy fights her own battles."

"Good answer. Is this a bad time?"

"No. Yvonne, Leo, and the kids went to brunch with your uncle Ewan and aunt Natalie."

Padraig grinned in such a way that Ryder knew he'd already timed his visit based on that intel.

"Which you knew."

Padraig didn't deny it.

Ryder sighed as he stepped aside, gesturing for Padraig to enter. "Your family has issues, man."

Padraig laughed as he walked in. "Probably, but you'll never hear me complain."

The two of them walked to the living room, Ryder making a detour by the kitchen to grab them both a beer. Of all Darcy's cousins, Ryder figured he'd probably spent the most time with Padraig, though only because the man served him drinks whenever he stopped by the pub for a beer with Leo or a happy hour with Darcy. They'd never had a serious conversation, their past chats limited to bourbon, sports, and the weather.

"Guess it's pretty obvious why I'm here," Padraig started once they were settled in the living room, Padraig on the couch, Ryder on the recliner.

"I'm sorry about last night, starting that shit in the pub. Let's just say that wasn't my finest moment."

Padraig shrugged and grinned. "It's an Irish pub, man. Believe me, yours wasn't the first fist to fly in there, and I'm sure it won't be the last."

Ryder took a sip of his beer. "Even so, I'm sorry."

"Yeah, well, the apology wasn't necessary, but it's

accepted just the same. Debated whether or not I should come over because I know what's going on between you and Darcy is none of my damn business. It's just...I've always sort of felt a kinship to you. If that makes sense."

Ryder nodded. While he didn't know Padraig well, he felt as if he knew him too. They'd both been widowed when they were young men. "It does. I've felt the same."

Padraig picked at the label on his beer bottle for a moment. "Everyone grieves differently, Ryder. And you can't work off anyone's timeline."

"I'm not still grieving for Denise."

Padraig looked up and studied his face—really studied it—and Ryder recognized the moment Darcy's cousin realized that was true. "Good. That's good."

And while Padraig acknowledged Ryder's misery had lifted, Ryder could also see Padraig was still swimming in a sea of it. Still devastated over the death of his wife, Mia.

"I didn't break things off with Darcy because of Denise's death. I broke them off because of her *life*. Our life *together*. I wasn't a good husband, Padraig. I worked long hours and even when I was home, I wasn't really here—always working on the house or zoned out in front of the TV. I was distant and cold and stressed out all the time. No romance. No flowers. No sweet words. I shut Denise out because I thought my damn paycheck and the fact I was home every night was enough to prove that I loved her. That I shouldn't have to say it all the time. Darcy deserves better than that."

Padraig tilted his head. "How old were you when you married Denise?"

"Twenty-four."

"And when did Clint come along?"

Ryder gave him a rueful grin. "Six months after the wedding."

"Do you think you would have married Denise if she hadn't gotten pregnant?"

Ryder had had a lot of years to consider that question, but he'd never spoken the answer aloud. Even now, he couldn't make himself say it. "I really liked Denise when we were dating, but we'd only been together a few months. After we got married and Clint came along, I loved her."

"That's not what I asked."

"No," Ryder sighed. "I wouldn't have married her."

Padraig leaned back on the couch and took a sip of beer, letting that response sink in. "You're putting the pieces together wrong."

Ryder frowned. "What?"

"You're envisioning your future with Darcy based on old information. You're setting her up with the old Ryder in your mind. You need to start looking at Darcy's relationship with this new Ryder. Ryder 2.0."

He laughed. "Ryder 2.0?"

"Yeah. The upgrade. You've got a decade's worth of experience—and what looks a hell of a lot like regret—under your belt. You're not the same guy Denise married. Not even close. Take what you know about yourself now and put that man with Darcy. Let's say you start dating, that you and Darcy get married. Does Ryder 2.0 still work all the damn time?"

Ryder shook his head. "No. I...wouldn't be able to wait to get home to her. Which is crazy when you consider we work in the same office."

"That's right. You do. What's work look like?"

Ryder grinned. "We'd take our lunch break together every day. I'd stop by her desk a couple dozen times a day to steal a quick kiss or just to see her."

"And when you're home? You zoned out?"

"It's hard to be zoned out around Darcy. She's got the Collins gift for gab."

Padraig chuckled. "Yeah. But that's her talking. What about you? You distant?"

"No. I tell Darcy everything. Can't seem to stop myself."

"Are you in love with my cousin?" Padraig asked.

Ryder's answer was instantaneous. "So much I can't fucking see straight."

"Do you trust her?"

Again, Ryder didn't hesitate to respond. He nodded, realizing that trust was the bigger-ticket item in his mind. Loving Darcy was easy. Hell, he'd probably fallen for her on that damn elevator at Halloween.

It was the trust that had been hard to give, to acknowledge because there was a lot of fear attached to that. Fear of setting himself up for heartache, of being hurt again, of losing Darcy.

Then he realized those fears weren't there anymore because he did trust her. Darcy wasn't Denise and she would never cheat, lie...leave.

"Yeah. I do. Completely."

"You and that Ron guy... You aren't strangers."

One of the reasons Padraig was a great bartender was because he was observant, a quick study when it came to people. Ryder had already noticed that about the other man, but it had also been pointed out by Yvonne and Leo and Darcy over the years.

"I know him. His daughter and my son, Clint, are in the same grade. They've been in classes together for years."

"Why did you punch him?"

Ryder swallowed heavily. For four years, he'd carried around this secret, and it had eaten away at him like cancer. Telling Darcy had started him on the road to recovery. He didn't want to go back to the man he'd been before that power outage.

"Ron and Denise had an affair. The day she was killed, she was leaving me to run off with him."

Padraig was quiet for a long moment. "Fuck. Didn't see *that* coming. I thought maybe he just owed you money."

Ryder laughed, grateful for Padraig's joke, for his attempt at lightening the tension with humor, even though his chest ached. "I found out she was leaving me the day she died. I didn't realize the other man was Ron until a few months after that."

"And you never confronted him? Not until last night?"

"Ryder 1.0 wasn't exactly the type to wear his heart on his sleeve. He played his cards close to his chest, never let anyone get too close. Safer that way."

"Safer. But a lot lonelier."

Ryder lifted one shoulder casually. "Yeah. It is. I loved Denise, but I wasn't *in* love with her. It wasn't the sort of passionate, all-consuming love that makes men compose symphonies, fight wars, or...punch out the other man. Besides, once I had the name... Oliver was right. Ron's a good guy."

Padraig scowled. "Good guys don't sleep with other men's wives."

Ryder held his hand up. "Fair enough. You're right.

You're absolutely right. They don't. But...I think he made her happy. I didn't." Ryder had seen a lightness in Denise those last few months before she'd died. Heard her singing in the kitchen, noticed she smiled more. He hadn't been the one to make her feel that way. Ron had.

"So you didn't punch him because of Denise?"

"No. I didn't. I saw him standing next to Darcy and..." Ryder ran his hand through his hair, the anger and frustration of last night returning to him in a rush. "Fuck, man. I saw red. She's mine. Darcy's *mine*. I just... Shit. I can't hurt her. I can't let her down. I can't do that."

"Then you won't." Padraig gave him a comforting grin. "It sounds to me like Ryder 2.0 is the kind of guy who does write symphonies and fight wars. And we know he punches out the other guy."

Ryder smiled...and the light went on. "Yeah. He does."

DARCY WALKED into the pub shortly before the dinner rush, ready to end this day the way she'd started it. Curled up in a ball in her bed, crying her heart out. She would actually still be there if Sunnie hadn't shown up just after lunch and dragged her miserable ass out to a salon for mani/pedis and haircuts. Darcy had been perfectly happy in her oversized flannel pajamas and messy bun, and she'd figured there wasn't enough makeup in the world to cover her puffy eyes.

But no amount of resistance would sway her sister, who said they were going to let the women at the salon work on the outside while the two of them worked on the inside.

She'd appreciated Sunnie's efforts, grateful to her sister

for letting her pour her heart out, allowing her to talk it all through. Dad had told her she had to be patient last night, something she sucked at, and she'd honestly expected Sunnie to countermand Dad's suggestion, to tell her to forge on. Actually, Darcy had been counting on that.

Instead, Sunnie agreed with Dad. Insisted that Darcy wait for Ryder to come to her. Something that was easier said than done, though Sunnie was convinced Darcy wouldn't have to wait long. She wished she had her sister's confidence, but Sunnie hadn't been there last night.

Hadn't seen Ryder's face.

Yvonne had shown up at the salon just as she and Sunnie were finished and dragged Darcy shopping. Darcy had been less resistant to her invitation, hoping for some kernel of information about Ryder's state of mind. Unfortunately, Yvonne hadn't seen Ryder since the incident at the pub. She'd fallen asleep early with the baby, and she and Leo and the boys had gone to brunch before Ryder had come out of his bedroom that morning.

They'd gone to a couple high-end boutiques, and Yvonne had even convinced her to buy a new dress, one that she'd actually worn out of the shop because Yvonne insisted that her outfit needed to match her hair and makeup.

Darcy had felt like an idiot, but she'd gone along with it because it seemed like the quickest and easiest way to get back home to her bed.

Darcy pulled out her cell and glanced at the screen for the four-millionth time today. No text. No missed calls.

Figures.

"All dressed up and nowhere to go," she muttered under her breath.

She glanced over and caught sight of Mom and Dad standing in the doorway between the pub and Sunday's Side. She was hoping they'd let her pass by without wanting to chat. Her bed was calling. Mercifully, they just waved and continued talking to each other.

That was when she spotted her brother, Finn, with Layla, Miguel, and Oliver, sharing a couple pitchers in a corner booth, all looking in her direction and smiling.

Dammit. Ryder was right. She had too much family. And the thirty-five steps from the front door of the pub to her apartment were going to be too many for her to make a clean escape.

"There's my pretty lass. Come keep an old man company."

Darcy glanced over to the bar and attempted a smile, one that went wobbly really quickly when she saw her Pop Pop pat the stool next to his.

She wiped away an errant tear as she approached and sat down, fighting hard to swallow down her sadness. Of course her grandfather didn't miss it, so he had his handkerchief out, ready for her.

"Dry those eyes, lovely girl. It would be a shame to mess up that fancy makeup."

Darcy took it and blotted her face carefully, though it didn't matter if she *did* mess it up. The only place she was going was to bed.

"Wine, Darc?" Padraig asked, walking over to them.

She shook her head. "Not tonight. I'll make some tea when I get upstairs."

Padraig reached over and gave her hand a squeeze. "Everything's going to be okay."

She appreciated the comforting words, but she wasn't feeling as certain as he and Sunnie.

"I heard about last night," Pop Pop confessed.

"Yeah. I've had better nights."

"I have a very good feeling everything will turn out okay. Jealousy isn't a weak emotion."

"Dad said the same thing. It's just...he's it for me, Pop Pop. The Collins curse took me down at twenty. I'm trying to be patient, trying to give him time to..."

"To?" Pop Pop prompted.

Before Darcy could reply, a deep voice behind them answered the question for her.

"To get his head screwed on straight."

Darcy twisted around on the stool and came face-to-face with Ryder—who was carrying an obnoxiously huge bouquet of red roses.

"To figure out that he's been a jackass," Ryder continued. "To recognize that he's walked away from the love of his life. The best thing that ever happened to him."

"The best thing..." she whispered, standing.

He nodded. Then he tilted his head, studying her. "You got your haircut."

She laughed, though the sound was mingled with some of those tears she'd been holding back. "Just a trim."

"I like it. And...I love you."

Darcy struggled to breathe. Her heart was racing, her palms sweaty, stomach twittery. "Ryder."

"I'm sorry about last night. And I'd like the chance to make it up to you. If you'll let me."

She smiled and nodded. "Okay."

He smiled back as he handed her the roses, then he took

her hand and drew her closer, stealing a quick kiss. Obviously, he'd noticed they were surrounded on all sides by her family.

"Do you mind if I steal Darcy, Mr. Collins?" Ryder asked.

"Not a bit, son. And for future reference, it's Pat. Or in your case, I think Pop Pop might work best."

Darcy didn't miss how moved Ryder was by her grandfather's words. Or how he glanced at Padraig behind the bar and gave him a quick nod and a smile. "Thanks, Paddy," he said.

"Paddy?" Darcy asked, surprised to hear Ryder use their family nickname for her cousin.

"You two get out of here and have a good time," Padraig said, reaching out to take the roses from her. "Hand me those and I'll put them in water, run them upstairs for you."

And that was when the light went on.

The hair, the makeup, the new dress, her parents hovering like two nosy old women…

"Everyone knew you were coming," she said as Ryder grasped her hand and led her to the door.

"They might have helped me set some stuff into motion."

Darcy was only two steps out of the pub when she stopped in her tracks and gasped. "Oh my God."

A stretch limo awaited them on the curb.

She laughed. "You got a limo."

Ryder tugged on the hand he still held and led her to the car. The driver got out, but Ryder waved him off. "I got it," he said.

Before he opened the door, he whisked her around,

pressing her against the side of the vehicle, and kissed her with so much passion, her head spun.

"I love you," he said again.

"I love you too."

"What's the Collins curse?"

Darcy frowned. "What?"

"I heard you tell your Pop Pop that the Collins curse took you down at twenty."

She laughed. "It's something Colm made up. He said the Collins family is all cursed because when we fall in love, it's fast, hard, and forever."

"And here I was thinking you'd put me under a spell." He opened the door and she climbed into the back of the limo, overwhelmed by the need to pinch herself to make sure this was all real.

Ryder handed her a champagne glass once they were inside, and the limo pulled away from the curb. He poured them both a glass of bubbly. "I'm afraid I had to make a few changes to your plan for the ideal date. Too many people live in my house and it was easier to move us than the baby."

She laughed. "I understand completely."

"So we're going out to dinner at this little Italian place near the waterfront. Then I've booked us a suite at a hotel, where we can dance and talk about our plans for the future, and then..."

"Sex?" she asked with a mischievous grin.

He shook his head as if disappointed. "So unimaginative."

Darcy shrugged. "What can I say? Compared to you, I clearly suck at romance."

Ryder took the champagne glass from her, placing them

both in a special holder before turning back to her. He wrapped his arm around her and drew her close. "Tell you what. You keep coming up with the plans and I'll carry them out. Speaking of which, I think this is the part where we get to make out."

She laughed. "At the beginning of the date? Scandalous."

He shook his head. "Nope. Nice."

"Feeling pretty sure of yourself," she teased.

"Not really. I wasn't sure you'd accept my invitation or my apology."

"I wasn't flirting with Ron."

"I know that, Darcy. I've never experienced jealousy before, and I reacted badly. Besides, Ron and I..."

Darcy waited for him to finish. He didn't.

And that was when she realized.

"Oh my God. It was *him*. Wasn't it? He and Denise—"

Ryder nodded. "His daughter is in Clint's class."

"I'm so sorry."

Ryder tightened the arm around her shoulders. "I'm not. Seeing you with him...it helped me pull my head out of my ass."

Her Pop Pop and her dad had mentioned similar revelations in the heat of the moment.

"So you got your revenge."

"No. I didn't punch him because of Denise. If it had been that, I would have hunted him down years ago. It's just what I said. I was jealous over *you*. Because you're mine. Just mine. From now on."

Darcy cupped his face with her hand. "That's all I've ever wanted to be."

He kissed her softly. "No more denials. No more secret dating. This is it. We're a couple. Facebook official."

She sniffled as one happy tear slid down her face. "I'm going to hold you to that."

"Tonight is for us. Just us. Then tomorrow, if you're willing, I want to tell Clint and Vince about us together."

"Are you sure?" she asked, touched, excited.

"Yeah. Never been more sure about anything. But I feel like I should warn you, Buttercup. I'm the kind of guy who dates with an eye toward marriage."

She laughed. "So noted."

"Can we make out now?"

EPILOGUE

"There's my girl. I was wondering when you would get here. How was the dance last night?" Pop Pop asked.

Darcy grinned as she entered his bedroom, winking at him as he tucked a bookmark into his romance novel and slid it under his pillow. "How dirty is this one?" she teased.

He chuckled. "It has a purple cover and an Irish heroine with long, flowing dark hair. Those never tend to disappoint."

Pop Pop was a huge fan of romance novels, his tastes turning to the historical variety lately, though he certainly wasn't picky. He'd also gone through paranormal and romantic suspense phases as well.

"The dance was amazing. Incredible. The hotel decorations were gorgeous, the whole place bathed in candlelight and white flowers. And the band was so good. Ryder and I danced the entire night."

She and Ryder had joined her cousin Caitlyn, and her

husband, Lucas, for a Valentine's Day dance at one of the hotels Lucas owned.

"Well, that sounds a lot better than your senior prom. No cardboard cutouts?"

Darcy laughed. "Mercifully, no."

"How's the move to Ryder's going?"

Darcy nodded. "Almost done. Clint and Ryder are actually over at the Collins Dorm as we speak, grabbing some boxes of books I'd packed up. Everything else is already at their place. I hadn't intended for all of this to go so quickly, but once we asked everyone how they felt about me moving in, Clint was a man on a mission."

"That boy loves you."

Darcy smiled, recalling how excited Clint was when she and Ryder told him they were dating. Since then, he'd moved her into what Ryder was calling the "mom" role, inviting her to his Christmas program at school, asking for help with his homework, and insisting she join him and Ryder the day they went shopping for new jeans because he'd outgrown all his pants. The kid had shot up two inches in just a few months. "I'm pretty crazy about him too."

"I've been waiting for you to get here. Wanted to show you my surprise."

Pop Pop had called her yesterday to ask if she would stop by. She never said no to a visit, especially when it was just the two of them in his room. She loved the times when she got him all to herself, rather than having to share him with everyone else at the busy pub or during family events.

Darcy realized she'd been blessed—luckier than her other cousins—because she'd grown up living in the same house with the beloved man. She had managed to steal more time with Pop Pop than most, simply because he was always there when she was younger, in the same house, day after day.

"I love surprises."

She followed Pop Pop to his special wall of photographs. Each member of their family was represented there, and it was her favorite place in the whole house. As a child, she'd sit on Pop Pop's lap, point to a picture at random, and he'd tell her a story about that aunt or uncle or cousin. Hour after hour of family stories, and he'd never repeated a single one. She liked to tease him that he knew all of their stories better than they did.

"Wait," she said, studying the wall. "My picture's gone."

"That's the surprise." Pop Pop picked up a frame from his nightstand. "You needed a new one."

Her previous photo had been in the frame since high school, a candid of her with her mom, Bubbles, and Sunnie the night of her senior prom. The four of them had been standing in front of the mirror in her bedroom, laughing hysterically as Sunnie helped her fix her hair for the dance. It had been such an unguarded, joyful, fun moment, and Darcy had always loved it because it was so reflective of her relationship with the three most important women in her life.

Darcy gasped when she saw what Pop Pop had replaced it with. "Where did you get this?"

"We knew Ryder was coming to the pub that night, so I asked your aunt Nat to do a little undercover photography for me."

Aunt Natalie was a professional photographer, and her

work was always breathtaking because she managed to capture so much in just one frame.

Somehow, unbeknownst to Darcy, her aunt had taken a photograph of her and Ryder standing by the limo, the night he'd whisked her away and told her he loved her for the first time.

Darcy wiped away a happy tear as she looked at it.

"You see it too, don't you?" Pop Pop asked.

She nodded and sniffled.

Ryder had her pressed against the side of the limo, and he'd just kissed her. She touched her lips because she could still remember exactly how amazing that kiss had felt, how wild and free she'd felt in his embrace.

In the photograph, she was blushing, smiling, and Ryder was looking at her like…

"That's a man who sees how extraordinary you are. Who can't imagine a single day of his life without you in it," Pop Pop said softly. "You found your true love."

Darcy turned then and wrapped her arms around her grandfather. "Only because you taught me what to look for. I love you, Pop Pop."

"And I love you, my lovely dark-haired lass."

DON'T MISS out on Oliver's story, Wild Dreams, coming April 2021. You can preorder it now!

HAVE you read the entire Wilder Irish series? All the books are standalone, so they can be read in any order. Be sure to check out all of them!

Wild Passion
Wild Desire
Wild Devotion
Wild at Heart
Wild Temptation
Wild Kisses
Wild Fire
Wild Spirit
Wild Side
Wild Night
Wild Embrace
Wild Dreams

FANS OF WILD Irish AND Facebook! There's a group for you. Come join the Wild Irish Facebook group for sneak peaks, cover reveals, contests and more! Join now.

BE sure to join my newsletter for a FREE Wilder Irish short story.

WILD DREAMS

Dream big. Dream wild.

Oliver has always longed for a love just like his parents have —all three of them. He's certain he's already halfway to that happily ever after. His foster brother calls it wild, but Ollie knows they can find the woman of their dreams.

Gavin has always accepted that life is just one disappointment after another. Growing up in the foster system taught him that. Oliver is one of the few people he can trust, so he prefers they stay a two-man band.

Erin is a curvy, spunky brunette neither of them saw coming. But fate has another wild card in store for the three of them, one that will test everyone's faith in their very different dreams for the future.

Preorder Wild Dreams now.

ABOUT THE AUTHOR

Virginia native Mari Carr is a New York Times and USA TODAY bestseller of contemporary erotic romance novels. With over two million copies of her books sold, Mari was the winner of the Romance Writers of America's Passionate Plume award for her novella, Erotic Research. She has over a hundred published works, including her popular Wild Irish and Compass books, along with the Trinity Masters/Masters Admiralty series she writes with Lila Dubois.

Find Mari Carr on the web at
www.maricarr.com
mari@maricarr.com

9 781958 056578